Remember a dream

Kara Lynn Amiot

Book one

Chapter one

Nhanni

I find it hard to remember a dream after I'm awake, even though my dreams have always been sharp and vivid. Some small corner of the mind always recognizes that a dream isn't real, but in the moment, it always seems like a tangible place. Most people are not agents in their dreams but a silent watcher hidden in invisible corners or gliding above the scene like a weightless body.

Silent.

But not me; I'm always myself in my dreams. I can see, hear, walk, touch…and speak.

I can talk in my dreams. That's how I know I'm dreaming. I have no voice, in real life. Once I wake in Arheynia, the world I grew up in, the world in which as a small child my voice was stolen from me by a sorceress, I can't speak.

I communicate by writing, and hopefully through a technique my professor, Adriyel, has been helping me with since I could cast my first spell. He's my personal mentor, according to my father's wishes, because it's too difficult for me to cast spells without words.

I'm probably the worst apprentice in Adriyel's class, and it doesn't please my father to see me struggle all because of a mistake he and mother made. They insulted and ridiculed a very powerful sorceress. Even the fact that it was unintentional didn't sway her from her desire for revenge.

It doesn't bother me, that I can't talk. Because , after all, I never could speak. Not since before I can remember.

Apart from in my dreams.

Apart from crooked scribblings in a worn, leather journal.

The loud clanking of a bell interrupted my writing, and I glanced up to the deserted halls. The wake-up bell. I still had time, but knew there was no harm in going to class early. I always had room to improve my *Mens Mentis Pulsus,* the technique Adriyel was working on with me.

The hallways were lined with sparkling white tiles, and long rays of light from the low morning sun cast across the floors through arched windows. This building was ancient, and I loved it. Millions of smooth stone blocks, carved to perfection with tiny flourishes and patterns, made up the walls and stairwells; the only things in the entire building *not* made of stone were the doors, desks, and bookcases.

I made it to the main hall, looked up, and sighed heavily. My stiff neck ached. It could take what felt like hours to reach the top of one of the winding stairwells. When I finally came to the last step, I took the first door on the left into a small ballroom. This building used to be an extremely large manor before it became an academy for magic apprentices, the same year during which the first royal sorcerer in history was chosen. There were not many of us at The Academy; magic was no longer common in Arheynia as it was hundreds of years ago. Back then nearly everyone possessed some magic ability, if only a tiny bit. Sometimes it was the most simple forms of magic which, when properly nurtured, grew into the most powerful. Now magic was rare, and very few had the talent and patience to pursue it, or so Adriyel said.

He was already at his desk when I arrived, his rectangular glasses nearly falling off the tip of his nose as he hunched over a leather-bound book, scribbling furiously.

"Good morning, Nhanni," he said, without looking up. "Ready to try your *Mens Mentis* again?"

I dropped my bag on a desk and sighed heavily, my way of telling him that I was certainly *not* ready, and perhaps never would be.

A smile pulled at the corner of his mouth. "I know it is frustrating, but practice makes perfect. Know that you have been doing well, Nhanni. It is not an easy technique for an advanced sorceress, let alone an apprentice. You must be confident."

I rolled my head back and sighed again, meeting his gaze.

"You think you are at the bottom of my class, but you must realize what you have already accomplished without the use of words. Spells are not easily cast without their words of power. You are much more talented than you think to have gotten this far without them."

He finished his scribbling and closed the massive volume over a ribbon. He removed his glasses with another smile and stepped from behind his desk. Adriyel was the king's sorcerer, the most powerful in all of Arheynia. He had come to The Academy to find a sorcerer or sorceress to be his successor, and to begin training the apprentices he believed had a chance of working for the king. It was probably because of him I'd made *any* progress at all. His magic was unrivaled, with the exception of the Oracle's magic.

Adriyel smiled, almost as if he could see these thoughts scrolling across my forehead. "I know you well enough to be able to tell what you are thinking. Even *I* cannot penetrate your mind unless you use this technique.

The power here comes from *you*. You are the one who must invoke *Mens Mentis Pulsus* and grant me access to your mind."

I finally nodded, released a long breath, and placed a hand on his arm.

"Try to give me something," he instructed. "Anything. How are you feeling?"

My eyes closed. My breathing slowed as I relaxed, letting my thoughts flow as effortlessly as I was able.

"Tired?"

I nodded, meeting his eyes again. I began feeding thoughts into his head, concentrating hard to keep my mind's natural defenses down.

"I see...the dreams again?" Adriyel asked after a moment. His voice became concerned with this reminder. His puzzled expression told me that he wasn't expecting my dreams to continue for this long.

Yes.

I finally managed to use a word. He smiled brightly and shook his head in surprise. "Tell me about it. What happened this time?"

My power began to falter, and my eyes closed again. I tried to summon more magic to tell him the rest. We both knew I wouldn't last much longer.

"Unfortunate. You could not remember this one either? Well, please let me know as soon as you do."

I nodded again. Adriyel nodded back to me to show I was done, and I sighed heavily as I released his arm. Forcing the brain's boundary down took an immense amount of magic, magic normally granted through the use of words of power - casting words. "Language grants us power", Adriyel always loved to say. But because I had no voice, I could never draw power the traditional way. I relied entirely on my own internal energy as a source.

Adriyel rubbed his chin thoughtfully, meeting my gaze. "Dreams are completely normal, even for mere mortals, so I wonder what it is about yours that puzzle me. Though deciphering dreams is a skill I have honed for much of my life, I have been able to decipher any dream but one of yours. They are strange to me."

The loud bell rang again. Classes would start in five minutes. I walked back to my seat.

Adriyel returned to his desk. "We will talk again at lunch. Perhaps the dream will return to you. You are using the journal?"

I nodded.

"Good. If you remember anything as you wake up, be sure to write it down before you forget."

The first student arrived a moment later, clad in the same blue uniform as me, and rubbing sleep from her eyes.

Adriyel glanced up. "Morning, Amberly."

She smiled at him, taking her seat, and gave me the same look everyone at this school gave me: a mix of pity and disgust.

The freak with no voice.

A sorceress unable to use words of power.

I sat patiently as the rest of them arrived, all of them yawning, fixing their hair, and straightening their uniforms as they sat. Taryn came jogging through the door, smiling brightly as he took the seat next to mine. His uniform, as usual, made his blue eyes seem even more vibrant, and his cheeks were red from running all the way here.

Taryn was the only friend I had in the class – if not the entire school - but Taryn was the type of friend you only needed one of. A best friend.

He yawned loudly, and I could tell that he had slept in by the way his sandy brown hair was swept aside in chaotic waves, and the fact that the bottom of his shirt wasn't tucked in.

"Morning. Did you finally sleep?"

I shook my head.

"Dreams again, huh? Is your *Mens Mentis* strong enough for you to show me yet?"

I was about to explain that I couldn't remember, when something came back to me. I now recalled that in one of my dreams I held a blade of browned grass that bloomed into a rose. Nothing about this dream seemed uncommon to me, but I reached for Taryn's hand anyway.

He placed his hand in mine, knowing automatically that I was going to show him. I took a deep breath, concentrating again on pushing my thoughts to the surface.

Taryn's eyebrows pulled together, as if he in turn was reaching for my thoughts but couldn't quite grasp them. "Sorry Nhanni. I don't hear anything. You're too tense."

I sighed, letting my eyes close. After a moment I could hear him gasp, and I met his blank eyes. He was watching the dream. His mouth, opened in a surprised 'O', which softened into a smile as the dream ended. He blinked and finally looked at me with a delighted expression.

"Wow! That's the first time you've ever been able to show me anything. Been working with Adriyel?"

I nodded.

"A blooming flower…did he know what it meant?"

I didn't remember the dream till just now. I'll tell him about it later.

Taryn jumped in his chair, his eyes even wider and his mouth popping open again. He stared at me a long time. "Did you just talk to me?"

I grinned in response.

He seemed unable to speak. Then, after a while, he laughed and released my hand. "Well…that's new."

The final bell rang and, to my disappointment, Jael actually showed up. He came strutting through the door and took his seat, his wandering eyes bright green, his hair jet-black.

He was the school's top student, and a favourite of the principal and professors who didn't have to put up with his attitude on a daily basis. Everyone knew him as the sorcerer the Oracle predicted would surpass Adriyel.

I knew him as the most arrogant, self-centered jerk I'd ever met.

Chatter filled the large ballroom, echoing loudly, until Adriyel stood from his desk with a look of authority about him. "That is enough. Class has begun."

When everyone fell silent, he lifted a stack of thick spellbooks, ignoring the students' groans as he passed them out. "I know. I know. But if you do well on this first quiz, we won't have to use these."

The room fell silent once again and he smiled in satisfaction. "Very good. Today I wanted to test your knowledge of spells." He raised his finger at Jael, who started to roll his eyes. "*And* their words of power."

Adriyel passed me an apologetic smile, since he understood how pointless this lesson would be for me. I sat back and prepared to do nothing the entire class.

"Words of power are the key to mastering spells. Without the energy of the word, the power does not exist," he explained, walking down the aisle of desks and handing each of us a spellbook. "Most of you don't know this, but language itself is magic.

Sorcerers such as yourselves are merely a vessel through which it can be expressed. Words provide a means for casting without relying on internal energy. While the power of the body is of a limited capacity, the power of words is truly infinite".

"This leads us to last week's lesson on the importance of names, and the reason why your true names are the key to gaining power over you," Adriyel added. "There is a reason none of you know your true names; it is to prevent other sorcerers from controlling you. Only the Oracle can reveal someone's true name, but words of power are known to all sorcerers."

He dropped the massive volume on my desk, its cover faded and worn with age. "It may help to think the word as you summon a spell," he told me, then paced to the front of the class. "This test is for everyone except Nhanni. You first, Garett. Why is it important to learn spells in pairs?"

"So we learn them twice as fast; save you some time?"

Adriyel put his hand on his hip and Garett grinned.

"It's because every spell has an opposite or a reverse. Spells that cause good are always balanced with spells that cause bad."

"Good. Amberly, your spells are creation and destruction. The word of power for creation?"

"*Creo.*"

"Destruction?"

She looked hesitant. "*Exitium?*"

"Yes. Good. Now you, Taryn. Give us a spell used to attack an opponent."

Taryn smiled at me, then winked. "*Incurro*. And a spell for defence is *Contego*."

"Well done."

Adriyel walked up the aisle of desks, then spun back around. His eyes seemed to be wandering with his brainstorming thoughts. "Sonya, state a pair of spells of your choice."

She was silent a moment, her head turned upward as she searched through her memory. "Invisibility and visibility; *Absconditus* and *Appareo*."

"Excellent," Adriyel said with a nod, looking pleased. " All of you seem to have been doing your reading for a change. Now, as we are nearing the end of the year, and your apprenticeship, it is important that you learn advanced skills such as these should the time arise for you to battle another sorcerer. Many of you will serve the king in the future, and you may look forward to further instruction from me on how to master such spells. For now, we must begin simply with practice. So, for the remainder of the semester I will be splitting the class into boy-girl pairs to do this."

The class groaned again, and I couldn't help but roll my eyes at their immaturity. *Oh please.*

Taryn groaned even louder, grinning at me when I glared.

"Alright class. *Alright*," Adriyel said calmly, meeting my gaze with a sigh of annoyance. "With your partners you will be competing against the other groups. Each team advances only when both partners cast a spell correctly. You don't have a choice. You must work as a *team*."

He grinned and grabbed Garett's pointed hat off his head, pulling folded pieces of parchment from his pocket and throwing them in. "Time to pick teams, kindergarten style. The names of the boys are in the hat."

He leaned against Sonya's desk and held the hat in front of her. "If you please."

She passed him an irritated glance and dipped her hand in, mixing the pieces of parchment around before pulling one out. Adriyel cocked his eyebrow at her disgusted expression. "Garett."

Garett glanced over his shoulder, giving her a nod and a wink. The entire class, including Adriyel, burst into laughter as she turned pink and covered her face with her hands.

Adriyel made his way towards Amberly and I glanced at Taryn nervously. If his name was chosen there was only one option left, and I didn't even want to think about that.

My life would be over.

Amberly reached in, took out one of the two remaining names, and read it aloud. "Taryn."

My breath escaped like a giant gust of wind as Adriyel pulled the last name from the hat. Taryn sighed loudly, shrugging his shoulders at me.

"And that leaves-" Adriyel said, glancing at me with another look of apology. "Jael."

I let my head fall against the desk. *Oh, confound it!*

Chapter two

Jael rolled his eyes dramatically and tapped his foot as Adriyel circled the ballroom. The desks had been carelessly pushed aside into one heap, and each team was practicing spells in the order of the textbook. The room sounded with the students' shouts of spells, and the gentle hisses as magic was released in technicolor flashes.

I had been practicing my *Creo* for a while now as Jael stood, waiting impatiently, the entire time. My brow wrinkled as I pushed magic from my hands, trying, and failing, to create something with the spell. Anything.

Jael glanced at me, and shook his head with an almost pitying look. "Of course...Adriyel probably planned to have you pick my name out of the hat. Knowing him, he purposefully put the best and worst student on the same team."

Unable to say anything in response, or even think of a reply, I turned away from him and tried to focus. If *he* was so wonderful, why didn't he help me with all these spells?

He sighed and continued to tap his foot until Adriyel came to us. "You first, Jael. Let me see it."

Jael gratefully spread his feet apart with a confident smile. "Any requests?"

"You want specific? Fine. An apple the exact size of my fist, perfectly juicy, half red and half green."

Jael cocked his eyebrow, glanced at Adriyel's fist, then raised his hands in front of him. "*Creo.*"

In a flash of green light, and with a wave of his hand, the apple appeared in his open palm. He held it out to Adriyel, who examined it with slightly wide eyes before taking it from his hand and biting into it. "Perfect. Just the way I wanted it. I should not have expected anything less from *you,* I suppose."

Adriyel turned to me with an encouraging smile. "Ready?"

I shrugged my shoulders and spread my feet apart, trying to hide that I was worried. I did my best to ignore the fact that Jael was even there. It didn't help my concentration to see his smug, condescending grin from the corner of my eye.

"Do your best," Adriyel said with a nod while Jael took a seat on the tile floor.

"Could take a while," he muttered.

I glared in his direction before raising my hands.

"Try something simple, Nhanni. Think you could create a clear glass?"

I nodded, my eyes already closed. I breathed deeply and cleared my mind before opening them again, waving my hand as Jael had. The harsh blue light nearly surrounded me, swirling and sparkling like stars. The power was almost overwhelming, and for a moment it filled me to the point that I thought I may explode.

Try as I might though, the glass did not appear. I could feel that the energy was surging within me, and yet it refused to convert to magic as I tried my best to summon it. After a moment, I gave up on the spell and let my hands fall, sighing in defeat.

Adriyel put his hand on my shoulder. "You are getting closer, Nhanni. Do not give up so easily. I will come back around and you can try again."

Jael groaned loudly to make his frustration with this clear, and Adriyel whirled around to face him. "And *you*…why not try helping your partner for a change?"

Jael's eyes widened. "You can't be ser-"

"The Oracle says you are destined to take my place? I expect it proven. Try teaching another student. We will see how easy *that* is for you."

Adriyel continued to the next group and Jael sighed again, rolling his head back. I could tell he expected Adriyel to be more cooperative, and didn't have any intention of helping me when he could simply weasel his way out of being my partner. I met his gaze expectantly, and he stared at me a long time before finally jumping to his feet. He seemed to have finally accepted that Adriyel had the authority here.

"Fine. Shouldn't be too hard; you weren't actually that far off."

This stopped my train of thought altogether. It was probably the nicest thing I had ever heard him say, to anyone, in all our years at The Academy. He wasn't exactly known for being the kind and complementing type. Most often, he emanated pure narcissism and made clear his dislike for learning alongside his classmates. It was as if he thought it beneath him.

He came up to me, running his hands through his hair as he thought for a moment. "When I was watching earlier, I noticed that you were trying to force your magic a bit. Because you can't speak, your magic comes from *Navitas Penitus*, internal energy, and forcing it out can actually block it. You're not at Adriyel's level you know...even if you're already learning an advanced spell. You have to master small amounts of magic before you can achieve anything close to what Adriyel can achieve. And unlike with most sorcerers, conserving your energy becomes a factor too. I think if you relax and let your energy flow inside you, a little bit at a time, you can summon your magic more easily. Make sense?"

He was actually *helping* me.

Even if I could speak, I wouldn't have been able to. I just nodded stiffly, too stunned to attempt the spell again.

He smiled slightly, and there was a short silence while we stood awkwardly and tried not to meet each other's gaze.

"Alright then. I guess...give it a try."

I once again focused my mind on the task at hand, letting my energy flow through me and fill me to the brim. Concentration was still difficult with Jael watching me so intently, and I saw him flash another grin when something I was doing caught his eye.

"See? Your whole body is still tense. Relax everything. Just breathe. How do you expect to harness your energy and cast a spell when you're hardly daring to draw breath? Think of your strength as coming from each breath itself."

My eyes closed and I waved my hand gently, sucking in more air as I did so. Unable to use words of power, I simply thought the word *Creo* over and over in my mind as Adriyel had suggested earlier. I opened my eyes to see familiar blue light surrounding my hands and, still skeptical that I would actually succeed, gave my hand one last flick.

The light brightened dramatically, like a burning star shrinks in the moments before it explodes, then vanished just as quickly. I felt the cool surface of the glass as it fell into my hand, and released a quiet gasp. After the light was gone, I stood frozen a long time, staring in wonder and surprise at the glass I'd created from pure magic. Somehow, with Jael's guidance, casting the spell became all but effortless to me.

Eventually, Jael stepped forward, smiling with apparent surprise. "Wow, that actually worked! You know Nhanni, you're not as bad a sorceress as I always thought you were."

My brow wrinkled. Thanks...I think...

Adriyel saw that I succeeded and came toward us. Jael couldn't help but laugh at my expression. "Sorry…I meant that as a compliment but it didn't sound like one."

A *compliment*?

I stared.

"That was wonderful, Nhanni!" Adriyel said. His eyes shone with joy and his voice came out slightly higher in his excitement. "See what you can accomplish when you have confidence in yourself?"

He turned to Jael next, his smile widening. "And *you*, when you are thinking of others and helping them, Jael? That just proves your attitude will not get you anywhere, but kindness will. Perhaps you are worthy of my position after all."

Jael rolled his eyes again, looking more like his usual self now that Adriyel was pointing out his kindness. "Can we move on to the next spell now? If Nhanni hadn't held me back I'd already be *done*."

Adriyel and I sighed at the same time, and he met my gaze with a look of disappointment. "Perhaps I spoke too soon…looks like power is all he cares about after all. Alright. The next spell is destruction. Get to work, you two."

He stepped away from us and raised his hands, which glowed with his brilliant red aura. "*Creo*."

In a flash of light, a small pedestal appeared with a glass, like the one I was already holding, resting on top.

Adriyel nodded to Jael. "You first."

Jael took his stance as Adriyel left us, breathing deeply. His eyes abruptly became calm and focused. It looked as if he was able to completely forget that I was watching from close by. "*Exitium.*" He raised his palm towards the pedestal, and instantly the glass shattered. The sound made me jump in surprise, and his grin reappeared. He stepped back, motioning me forward to take my turn.

I glanced at the pedestal, then at the glass in my hand, and his smile spread when he caught on to what I was planning. "I'll get it." He raised his hand toward mine, swinging his arm in an arc toward the pedestal. "*Amitto.*"

The glass vanished right before my eyes, and, as I thought, when I glanced at the pedestal, the glass was on top of it.
I met Jael's gaze with an open mouh. I didn't understand till now that Jael actually had good reason for thinking so highly of his abilities.

"A sending spell. Piece of cake," he said.

Feeling slightly less confident about my power, I took my stance with my eyes locked on the glass. I raised my hand, and immediately relaxed when I noticed my arm was tense yet again. Blue sparks appeared at the base of the glass, flicking on and off as my concentration shifted, but nothing else happened for some time. I started to think the spell would fail again when the glass finally shrieked and shattered like Jael's had. I let my hand fall and met his gaze.

His eyebrow was raised. "Nice. Took you a while, though."

I rolled my eyes and, to my surprise he actually grinned.

"Well…" he said after a moment. "Guess it's onto the attack spell, as soon as Adriyel comes back, that is. Looks like we're ahead of the other teams now."

He glanced at me, and in place of his usual arrogant smirk was a soft smile. "Good work, partner. I wasn't sure you'd be willing to follow my advice, but you noticed how tense you were right away that time."

I stood frozen after he said this, and he turned to watch the other teams without noticing my reaction. Most of them were still struggling with *Creo*, and some with *Exitium*, and others were still waiting for Adriyel to come around.

After a moment, I walked to Jael's side and hesitantly placed a hand on his shoulder. My face fell when he jumped and glanced at me with a shocked expression, as if he hadn't noticed that I'd moved.

I tried my best to smile. Thank you for helping me.

He looked even more shocked. "*You* can use a *Mens Mentis Pulsus*? I didn't know that. That's not half bad, weakling."

I shrugged and he finally returned my smile, laughing lightly. "Everyone in this school seems to think you're an outcast simply because you have no voice, and because you have struggled to summon magic without the use of words, but it appears they couldn't be more wrong. You are just full of surprises, Nhanni."

So are you.

I had never spent five seconds with Jael, and I was starting to see that even though he only cared about how powerful he was, and how much others admired him, he wasn't as hard as he wanted others to think he was. I saw a different side, one who was genuinely happy to see someone besides himself succeed and to have played a part in making it happen.

I shook my head in disbelief at this realisation. You're not as much of a jerk as I always thought you were either.

He met my gaze again, his brow wrinkled. He obviously wasn't used to this kind of compliment, and wasn't sure how to reply.

Thanks again, Jael.

The lunch bell rang through the halls and he shrugged my hand off, but a smile was pulling at the corners of his mouth. "Whatever. You're welcome, I guess."

I started to eat my own lunch, and our gazes turned to the door as Jael returned with a large group of people following him. Most of the guys were athletes (although this was not a mortal academy, the professors thought it was important for students to be active in something other than magic once in a while), and all of them seemed to have a girl on his arm except Jael. For some reason I couldn't comprehend, this intrigued me.

After a moment, I turned back to Taryn, taking his hand. *I wonder why Jael is never with girls.* As much as I disliked him, even I could admit that he was very good looking. 'Till now, I had never noticed that he didn't girlfriends, or even friends that were girls.

Taryn raised his eyebrow at me. He looked like he was wondering what would posses me to ask such a question. "You don't know? Didn't you ever wonder why Adriyel never got married?"

I couldn't help but become confused when he mentioned Adriyel. What did *he* have to do with this?

"Adriyel has been mentoring Jael as well as you," Taryn explained, when he noticed that I didn't understand. "Preparing him to take his place and all, because of the prophecy."

I nodded for him to continue.

"Well when Adriyel became the royal Sorcerer, he was very in love with a girl. He'd been friends with her all through their years at The Academy, and they became very close the year that they graduated, so I've been told.

One time, he was locked in a serious conflict with another sorceress and defeated her, but made the mistake of sparing her life. This other sorceress was angry about being defeated, and murdered the girl Adriyel loved simply out of spite."

My eyes widened. *What?*

For someone to do such a thing was incomprehensible; killing an innocent girl for no reason other than because she was beloved by an enemy.

"Yeah…apparently Adriyel came very close to quitting and giving up magic forever, even though everyone knows how much it is frowned upon. My guess is, now that Jael is meant to take his place, Adriyel told him not to make the same mistake. Jael has probably been told many times, by others and not just Adriyel, that his emotions make him weak and in order to fulfil his duties he cannot have attachments to anyone. *Especially* a girl. Love has come to be seen as a vulnerability for people in such high positions, one that enemies will not hesitate to take advantage of. Even the royals, who are mortal and have no magic, rarely ever marry for love."

I glanced in Jael's direction again as I pondered an eternity alone. *That's awful. I wouldn't wish that on anyone, even Jael.*

"Don't know who would ever love that jerk anyway," Taryn muttered. "He probably thinks no one here is good enough for him."

I watched Jael a moment longer before I realized that I was staring and released Taryn's hand so I could get back to my lunch.

Adriyel approached us from his desk, pulling up another chair and taking a bite of his sandwich. "So, how was your first day of training?" he asked the both of us.

Taryn smiled, ignoring me when I gave him another disapproving glance. I could already predict what he was most likely to share with another man. "Well if you mean 'How did my partner and I get along?', just fine. Unfortunately, her progress was slow, and we're still stuck on the creation spell."

"I saw that both your glasses were shattered," said Adriyel, as he turned to me. "Seems you and Jael are doing even better than Taryn's team."

"Nhanni thinks he's *nice*," Taryn informed him, rolling his eyes at me. He still wasn't over it, it seemed.

"I believe it. That boy is under a lot of pressure because of the Oracle's predictions. The entire kingdom has such high hopes and expectations now, so it's no surprise that his family accepts nothing but the best from him. It is a big responsibility, and he puts up a hard shell, but underneath he is kinder than most people realize."

Taryn snorted again, and Adriyel glared coldly in his direction. "*I* would know…I am his mentor, and have been for a long time now. He's a great boy, but he is so obsessed with living up to everyone's expectations that he won't let anyone in. It's probably for the best, I suppose. With no emotional attachments, not even to his family, his enemies will have no way to threaten him."

Taryn continued eating, apparently unfazed by Jael's lonely fate, and I stared at the surface of the desk until Adriyel finally cleared his throat.

"So, you said that Nhanni *told* you," he began in a lighter tone, smiling brightly at me. "Your *Mens Mentis* is getting stronger, even since this morning. Seems Jael was a great help after all, just as I suspected he would be. Did you remember anything from your dream?"

Looks like the name draw was jinxed after all, I thought to myself as I remembered what Jael said. Typical Adriyel.

I nodded to Taryn, indicating that I wanted him to explain.

"Yes she did," he replied for me. "In her dream she held a piece of withered grass and watched as it bloomed into a rose."

Adriyel looked surprised, his gaze turning to me now. "Really? A dream I can finally decipher."

My face brightened and he nodded. "Yes, I know what it means. It is quite amazing, almost unbelievable, but your dream foretells a big change in your life."

"That's *impossible…*" said Taryn. His eyes held a look of doubt. "Not even sorcerers like *you* have dreams that see into the future."

Adriyel chuckled at Taryn's expression. "Some do, but it is exceedingly rare. It has only happened twice in my lifetime," Adriyel told him, before he glanced back at me.

"The withered grass symbolizes the end of your dependence on yourself, and the blooming flower represents change; the start of something new." His expression abruptly turned teasing. "The fact that it is a *rose* suggests a romance."

I felt my entire body tense at the shock of this.

So did Taryn's, from what I could see. "*What?!* Nhanni is going to fall in love? *Nhanni?*"

"It appears so, yes" Adriyel replied, appearing unimpressed with Taryn's obvious surprise. "Let me see, Nhanni."

I reluctantly gave him my hand, and his eyes closed as he watched the dream. A small hint of a smile pulled at the corner of his mouth. His amusement with this prediction annoyed me more than I was willing to let on, or it would only amuse him more.

"Yes…beautiful," Adriyel mused as he opened his eyes again. "By the looks of the rose, it will be a powerful love indeed."

I could feel my face getting hot as I pulled my hand away.

Adriyel cocked his eyebrow. He'd picked up on my desire that we drop the subject fast. "You don't believe me?"

I just stared at the desk, trying to avoid his gaze.

"Fine. It will happen soon enough." Adriyel continued to eat, but I could feel Taryn's eyes on me for what felt like an eternity before he also turned back to his meal. He'd known me since we were five, when I started my apprenticeship, and he was probably just as shocked as *I* was by this.

Based on his concentrated expression, I could guess that he was likely running through names in his head wondering who my future lover could possibly be.

He knew I had never even thought about boys before, and didn't ever consider that someone might like me that way. I was an outcast, after all, and I wasn't pretty like Amberly and the others. And I wasn't an athlete. I wasn't talented in anything besides magic, and even *that* was proving more and more difficult it seemed. Today was the first day I made any progress at all.

The thought of romance had just never occurred to me. Why would anyone like *me* that way? With a sigh, I glanced up at Taryn. In typical guy fashion, he was oblivious to my staring and too preoccupied instead with the meal in front of him. His eyes were cast downward, but I could still see a speck of blue beneath his thick eyebrows. I had always thought he had such pretty eyes for a boy. Though his hair was messy and his uniform had been sloppily thrown on, I noticed, today of all days, that Taryn wasn't bad looking…not at all.

In fact, he came close to matching Jael in looks.

As if finally sensing that I was staring, Taryn turned to me, his smile spreading.

I blushed and quickly lowered my eyes.

That did *not* just happen.

I definitely *did not* just have those thoughts about my best friend.

Chapter four

Raveena

1 month later

It wasn't until dark that my expected visitor finally arrived. He appeared from the shadows almost out of mist, once again the hood of his deep purple robe hanging down and covering the majority of his face. No one had ever seen him without his face covered. Now the cloak was almost as recognizable as the tall staff he always carried with him, the surest sign that he was not simply powerful, but dangerously powerful.

I could sense his aura right away. The pure energy surrounding him was so overwhelming that I automatically stepped several feet away from him, scrunching my nose.

I sighed loudly and swung open the door to the house, leaving it ajar as an invitation for him to come inside. "Normally I would be polite and offer you something to eat or drink, but you've kept me waiting long enough so I will skip the formalities."

"Very well," came a deep voice from the hooded figure. "You have never been patient, sorceress, but you are powerful. It must not have been easy to find me."

"It wasn't," I said roughly, though he intimidated me more than I cared to admit. I led him around the corner into my favourite room of the house, where a tall fireplace roared with flames that I could feel warming my skin from all the way across the room. "But you already knew that; it's exactly what you were hoping for. As the Oracle, you prefer to remain out of reach of those you do not want to confront."

I could see his mouth, partially hidden in the shadow of his hood, tilt up into a smile. "Of course I was avoiding you. You have done nothing but terrorize the people of Arheynia since my prophecy became known; the one you have become much too keen on manipulating to your advantage. And I thought that I made it very clear last time that the information I gave you was all you would receive. I have no intention of revealing any more now that I know what it is you hope to accomplish."

"Terrorize? What can you possibly mean?" I asked with the slightest hint of a teasing tone. It was the only way I could forget how truly terrified of him I was.

"You deliberately disobeyed me when you stole the child's voice, and continue to disobey me when you attack innocent sorcerers. You have placed yourself at the center of a prophecy which never had anything to do with you. No one in this land is a threat to you."

My anger was starting to overshadow my fear. I whirled around to face him, clenching my fist tightly at my side to keep my wild magic at bay. "Every *single one* of Adriyel's apprentices is a threat! As they continue to grow stronger and stronger it seems more unlikely that the prophecy will come to pass!"

He sighed heavily to himself; he sounded strangely human for an Oracle. "I have already told you, sorceress. Prophecies cannot be tampered with, and will come to be no matter how many times fate is challenged. It is just as it was seventeen years ago, when you first summoned me. You have no reason to fret over the inevitable, nor can you write your own ending into a future which has already been set."

I turned once more and watched the violet fire flickering in the fireplace, brushing my dark hair over my shoulder. I would not give him the satisfaction of seeing frustration and the smallest flicker of doubt on my expression. "Say it again."

Another sigh followed.

"The sorcerer to wield *Dust of the stars*
And all the power it may bring
Shall earn a place on a palace thrown
As sorcerer of Arheynia's king"

"*Dust of the stars*," I repeated to myself with a grin. "The medallion."

"The very jewel that the boy has had since the beginning. He is destined to serve the king, as you well know. I thought it was what you wanted, for Adriyel's service as royal sorcerer to come to an end."

"Jael is now in line to become the next royal sorcerer, and the people of Arheynia no longer suspect me. They no longer anticipate that I will make a move," I replied, my smile spreading as the bright light of the fire cast a glow over me. Its heat seemed to grant me newfound energy and power. "It's exactly what I want."

The Oracle was completely silent. I could not even make out the sound of his breathing as I glanced out the window. The sky was now black; no star or moon in sight. "Many have boasted of their family's power, and have paid the price for it. For too long, families like Adriyel's have had their place on the throne and helped to govern the kingdom as they saw fit, but soon…very soon *I* will be the royal sorceress and have complete control."

The wind began howling outside, sending leaves and fallen twigs flying against the windows with alarming noise. The Oracle's voice, usually so unnaturally calm and quiet, raised to a menacing roar. His aura's energy grew more than overwhelming now, overflowing and filling the room nearly to the brim with its strength and power. "Do not even think about going anywhere *near* the boy! Too many have already fallen victim to your cruelty and treachery...namely Nhanni!

You cannot go around harming every family or sorcerer that becomes more powerful than you. No matter what you do, the throne will never be yours. It is written. It is seen. You cannot expect that linking your life to the boy's life will link your futures as well."

I met his gaze, heat rising to my cheeks. I couldn't stop my temper from taking over, and I knew by the violet flames flickering at the tips of my hair that I was moments from losing control. Magic was surging through me, fueled by hate. "The throne *will* be mine. My plan has already begun to succeed. Would I have brought you here if I believed you stood any chance of stopping me? My purpose in summoning you is to boast, oracle, and nothing more. To show you and the other rulers of this kingdom what happens when you cross me."

I expected a show of temper from him in response, but his deathly silence was all the more frightening. He stood still as death while the night howled outside. His mouth, the only visible feature, showed no emotion or response even when he finally spoke.

"I have seen, for a long time, that you are foolish enough to doubt the word of the Oracle. Do not flatter yourself in presuming that I came here simply because you summoned me. I answer to none but the king. I came to warn you that if this treachery does not stop now, you will get what is coming to you."

My eyes narrowed as I glanced away. The heat from the tall fireplace was beginning to burn my eyes, but I stared and the flickering images taking shape before me as I thought.

Neither of us spoke for a long while, and there was nothing to fill the silence but the soft sound of sparks.

When the Oracle realized I wouldn't respond, he continued. "The power you seek can never be yours. The future is set. My purpose in showing myself once more is not to give you hope, but to remind you of what I told you seventeen years ago. You have already lost. You would be locked in a cell if you did not have the girl's voice, her very life, in your grasp. If you harm anyone else, especially Jael, you will answer to me. Heed my words this time, sorceress. It is no idle threat."

I turned away from him, rolling my eyes at this dramatic speech.

"You do not fear even *me...*" the Oracle said with a slightly surprised voice. "Then perhaps it is Adriyel and the Royal Army you fear?"

I stiffened noticeably, despite myself, and heard a faint chuckle in response. "That is what I thought. Do not call on me again, sorceress. This will be your last warning."

As always, when I turned back to face him he was gone. "Yes, I know...the prophecy will come true," I said to myself now, my grin returning at the thought of his foolishness. "That's what I am counting on."

Chapter five

Nhanni

What can be seen in someone who can't express themselves? In the beginning, voices reached me from what felt like a universe away, a place where thought could rule over physical words. Only now did I really start to hear them, and only now did they start to hear the soft whisper of my speechlessness.

Maybe more is said with silence.

Maybe the jumble of sounds that come across as words to people's ears only distorts the message behind the voice. Maybe more is said from inside, from the depths of the hearts oceans, rising up slowly like soft bubbles of air yearning for an escape.

They can better hear the melody in their ears, but if they listen closely enough they can find soft harmonies trying to push through.

Beautiful harmonies that show understanding, harmonies that whisper the answers they never searched for, but they can only hear the melody long before the song even plays.

True beauty is always hidden.

It can never overpower illusion, can never break the glass dome of the heart, the gateway preventing unwanted intruders from entering inside.

Why do people put up that gate?

Why do they exclude the unknown, the truly terrifying truly beautiful mysteries surrounding them, and only let in the things they know? They let in the lies, the betrayals, the masks, the glories , and the melodies.

They can never find harmony, they can only find the loudest voice. The voice of an illusion pounding in their ears like bells, the shrill notes capturing their attention from any noise in the background.

They can only find the loudest voice, while beauty's mute whispers fall into the unknown...in the one place no one ever thinks to look.

In some ways simplicity is more beautiful than splendor, I think. A mere smile can be considered more beautiful than polished diamonds. One act of kindness can be a greater gift than all the riches in the world.

Simplicity should be treasured, recognised, and appreciated past all the rest. Sometimes simplicity is what is best for us, in times when we feel disconnected or lost, as if we are in a dream.

Simplicity feels real; it feels right. It is the beauty we do not have to work at or search forever to find...we can just let it be: eyes catching a sparkle of moonlight, that gentle breeze like a brush of silk, and a child's outrageous laughter.

It is beauty that was always meant to be, that we do not strive for, and that we do not have to look beyond.

There is beauty in life; in everything you look at but do not always see. There is beauty in growth, and change.

Life changes.

It shifts, fastforwards, reverses, and stands still in frozen moments. It is altered, remastered, and reimagined with melodies, words, and painter's hands.

But beauty stays the same.

It is nothing more or less than what we are given; it is just the way things are. Beauty is simply simplicity, and simplicity is simply beautiful.

I closed my journal just as the shrill ring of the bell alerted me that lunch was over. Releasing a heavy sigh, I slid the book back into my bag before walking to the center of the room, where the rest of the class was already waiting for Adriyel to return. Apprentices from other classes left quickly as he walked through the door, still eating his lunch.

"Get to class, all of you. If you have professor Eldyn right now, I suggest you come up with a very good lie."

When the doors to the ballroom closed, he smiled at us and dropped one of his huge spellbooks on his desk. "Get into your teams, everyone. I will come around and give each pair a final test to determine the winners of this challenge. Practice while you wait."

Jael turned to me as we walked to our corner of the room, smiling with confidence. "It's in the bag. Want to try the invisibility spell one last time before he comes? That one was the toughest for you, if I remember correctly."

I nodded, and Jael grabbed one of the wool dolls our class used for practicing spells. There were small black stains on the fabric of the dolls, singe marks from hundreds of spells. Jael gently set it on the floor a few feet away from me then took several steps back.

I raised my hand towards the doll, breathing deeply, focusing my magic. Both Jael and Adriyel had made a note of my improvement in summoning magic. Jael suggested that all I had left to learn was how to best focus my magic on a particular intention. At first, only small specks of blue light appeared, floating from my fingertips before slowly dying out. I sighed in frustration.

"Relax. You can do this, Nhanni. You've done it before."

I took another deep breath, but froze when someone's laughter echoed through the room. I turned toward the sound, and recognized the boy who was laughing as one of Jael's friends. Two of the stragglers from other classes had stayed behind to watch.

"Take a look at this, Morahn," one boy called to the other. "A sorceress with no voice. *This* should be interesting..."

I dropped my hands, turning my red face away as he laughed again, hiding my shame.

"Stop it, Gabe," Jael said.

I glanced back at him, unable to hide my surprise at his interference.

Jael's face was harder than usual. "It's not like she can help it."

Gabe and Morahn appeared both surprised and confused. Before either of them could speak, Adriyel approached from behind them. He grabbed the back of their sweaters in tight fists, and pulled them roughly towards the doors. "Out of my class, *now!*"

Jael sighed and glanced back at me. My eyes were still downcast. "It's okay, Nhanni. Keep trying."

After a moment I raised my hands again, my confidence growing when blue light appeared more vibrant than before. Anger could be a strong source of energy to fuel magic. I decided to make use of it. I took a deep breath and flicked my wrist, causing the light to spiral towards the doll. Almost too easily, it vanished.

Jael looked stunned. "That was fast! I told you you'd get it!"

I was surprised myself by how efficiently I was able to use casting the spell as an output for my anger. I glanced at him with a smile. After a month of spending every class with me, he recognized this as my 'thank you' expression.

"You're welcome," he said with a grin.

Adriyel returned from the hallway, stomping in anger. "I heard what Gabe said. Are you okay, Nhanni?"

I nodded, and for once I really meant it.

"Good. Thank you for that, Jael."

He shrugged, all signs of emotion gone just as quickly as they'd appeared. "It was nothing. Let's get started."

Adriyel cocked his eyebrow before turning to me with a grin, and a teasing look in his eye. "I saw a young man from Eldyn's class watching you at lunch. Maybe *he* is loverboy, huh Nhanni?"

My cheeks reddened automatically and I glared at him.

Jael noticed my embarrassment, and glanced at Adriyel with a confused expression. "Loverboy?"

"Yes. Nhanni had a prophetic dream not long ago. I could see a romance in her future."

"Really?" Jael said, his eyes wide. "But I thought only an Oracle could see the future."

"It is true, prophetic dreams are rare for mere sorcerers. It has happened before, to only a few individuals though. It must be that the universe is trying to tell you something, Nhanni," Adriyel said with a grin, then more quietly to Jael. "She does not believe me though."

I folded my arms and rolled my eyes dramatically, making Adriyel laugh.

"Alright…you ready?"

I nodded, afraid I'd back out if I waited.

He flashed a smile, before waving his hands around him in a smooth motion. "*Creo.*" Red light swirled like a flickering flame and pedestals appeared in a circle around me, each with objects on them specific to each spell. Once the light died down, Adriyel turned back to me. "Creation spell first."

I watched him nervously as he paced. "Let me see…how about an apple? The exact size of my fist, perfectly juicy, half red…"

I glared, and he laughed outrageously. "I am *kidding*. Try a soft cover book, made from red leather."

I raised my hands toward the empty pedestal, and my hands flashed with light as I summoned my magic. The book appeared, exactly as I had imagined it in my mind, and Adriyel nodded. "Good, you are improving. Next."

I turned to the pedestal with a clear glass on top, narrowing my eyes in concentration. I smiled to myself when the glass shattered.

"Good. Next."

I stole a quick glance toward Jael, who flashed an encouraging smile.

As I turned to the next stand, throwing the attack spell at the wool doll, Adriyel walked to the open space between two pedestals. The doll exploded in a flash of light, sending tuffs of wool and cotton flying in all directions.

"Fantastic. Nice job, Nhanni."

I couldn't help but tense when I realized which spell was next, and Adriyel smiled when he noticed. "You'll be absolutely fine, I promise. Jael, can you supervise for me?"

"Sure."

Adriyel nodded to me and I raised my hands again.

"It is just a defence spell, do not worry. Jael is watching so nothing will happen if the spell fails."

I breathed deeply, trying to keep from shaking, and Adriyel raised his hands. "*Incurro.*"

His red magic sped towards me like lightning, flickering in twists and spirals as if it were alive. I spread my hands defensively to summon a shield, but they didn't begin to glow no matter how hard I tried.

I looked away.

Familiar green magic appeared before me at the last moment, blocking the spell like a tall wall of light, and Adriyel relaxed. "Well done, Jael."

I breathed a sigh of relief and glanced in Jael's direction again. Thank you, I thought, even though he couldn't hear me.

"You're doing great. Try again."

Adriyel took his stance, and waited for my nod. "*Incurro.*"

I raised my hand towards the attack and the red light was drowned out by an intense blue glow. I squinted through it and held my ground, almost being blown over by the force of the magic coming from my hand.

After a moment, the light grew faint again and I glanced at Adriyel, who just stared at me with unnaturally wide eyes. I was uncertain about whether that was supposed to happen, or if I'd perhaps overdone it a little bit. I turned to Jael after a moment, and he grinned, raising his hands palm up. "It was *you* that time. Nicely done!"

"Yes," Adriyel agreed, looking overwhelmed. "That was a *very* bright glow. Well, moving on…"

I turned to the pedestal for the next spell, where another wool doll was sitting. I took a deep breath and directed my magic towards the doll, remembering the way I'd practiced the spell earlier. It vanished from sight in a flash, and I jumped in surprise.

"Yes!" said Jael excitedly, both of us breathing a sigh of relief. I had the sudden urge to giggle, but the image of Amberly flashed through my mind and instead, I shuddered.

The next pedestal appeared empty, and at first I forgot which spell was next. Then, when it finally came back to me, I used the visibility spell to reveal another wool doll.

"Great, Nhanni. Summoning and sending next."

I raised my hand towards the clear glass, refracting the light of my magic, and drew the hand back towards me as if grabbing it. The glass vanished and reappeared in my hand almost instantly. I stood stunned, then met Jael's surprised expression, before grinning and pushing my arm back forward. The glass returned to the pedestal and Adriyel nodded in approval. "Perfect. Keep going."

The last two spells.

I turned to the next stand and the blue light of my magic surrounded the doll like a cloud. I touched my fingers and thumbs together, creating a circle with my hands, then pulled my hands outward.

The doll grew.

"Yes, Nhanni! Well done!"

I closed my hands again, my mind feeling like a tense elastic band as I concentrated, and the doll shrunk back.

Adriyel's expression was so ecstatic I couldn't help but return his smile. "Wonderful! Just wonderful! You have improved so much, Nhanni. You completed the challenge on your first try! And well done remembering all your forms as well!"

Jael came into the circle to switch with me, smiling hugely when I met his gaze. "Great job partner. We're about to win."

Adriyel grinned at him before taking his stance. "I thought you might want to try beating the record. Are you up for it?"

"Who set it?"

Adriyel's grin spread He was expecting this question. "Me."

"Yes," Jael replied right away, taking his stance. "*Oh yes.*"

"*Creo,*" Adriyel said again. "*Exitium.*"

All the objects that had been destroyed or altered were replaced, appearing in puffs of red magic, and the journal I had created disappeared. "Best of luck. Go!"

Green light manifested from Jael's hands and flew around the circle in wavelike patterns, glowing so intensely I had to squint as I watched. I hadn't noticed before that every time Jael used magic, the medallion around his neck, set with a large gem, would glow as well.

Everything happened really fast.

Jael was shouting spells out more quickly than I could keep up, and moving from one pedestal to the next in what seemed like milliseconds.

The journal appeared, the glass shattered, and the doll exploded the moment he turned to them. Adriyel attacked Jael more quickly than I thought possible, but was easily blocked, and Jael continued around the circle without so much as a pause. One doll disappeared, the other appeared, the glass was in and out of his hand before I could blink, and I didn't even see the last doll grow or shrink before Jael shouted "Time!".

Adriyel was staring at him now, his face pale.

"Well? How much was that?"

"About seven seconds."

"Did it beat your record?"

Adriyel's eyes were very wide. "By a *mile*."

Jael turned to me as I entered the circle, grinning ear to ear as he laughed. I smiled, back and we high-fived each other like little kids. "Yes! We win, Nhanni!"

Adriyel, watching us, coughed to hide a laugh. "Not exactly...Taryn and Amberly beat you to it."

I glanced at Taryn from across the room, and he waved with an amused expression on his face when he saw me. I glared, folding my arms across my chest.

I turned back to see Jael's face fall. "What?"

"I was surprised too...Taryn's magic is just extraordinary," Adriyel replied, grinning at Jael teasingly. "He could teach even *you* a thing or two."

Jael gave him a look then, to my surprise, he laughed again.

"That's okay," he said, his smile reappearing as he turned to face me. "We'll destroy them next time."

"It will not be long until you get your chance. Eldyn and I are combining classes for sparring."

Jael's eyes widened. I couldn't tell if he was excited or surprised. "Real fights? Against *each other*?"

Ariyel sighed. "*Practice* fights."

"That sounds-"

"Like a really, really bad idea," Adriyel finished for him. "But sparring is mandatory once apprentices reach the age of eighteen; it is important that you all learn how to defend yourselves if you are to become the king's sorcerers. But sparring starts only after the rest of the teams are done this challenge."

The final bell rang, and Jael glanced up in surprise. "Great! I'll be late for my evening class with Eldyn! He told me to leave early!"

"Better get going," Adriyel told him. "Do me a favour and give your *friends* a talking to. They have no reason to be here if it is just to give Nhanni a hard time."

"Sure thing."

Jael quickly shoved his books in his bag, turned to leave, then glanced back at me. "Don't let any of those guys bother you, okay?"

I nodded, and felt my cheeks turn red when he flashed a lopsided smile.

Jael waved to me and Adriyel as he ran out the doors. "See you tomorrow!"

"Well that was…weird," Taryn said, making me jump as he appeared at my side.

I took his hand. *What?*

"That look he was giving you."

I stared at him a moment, confused, and he smiled as he raised his arm. "*Advoco.*"

My bag appeared in his hand and his grin spread as he slung it over my shoulder. "Do you care where we eat tonight?'

I shook my head.

"Good," he replied, taking my hand again. "Cause I know where we're *not* going."

Where?

"By the lake."

I cocked my eyebrow as he led me through the doors, avoiding my gaze. Something told me he had a secret. He always hid his eyes when he simply wasn't telling me something.

"The athletes eat there after school now," he explained.

Oh, I said, wondering to myself whether he was avoiding Jael or his so called *friends*.

Chapter six

Taryn

I entered the ballroom to see Adriyel sorting through stacks of old books, his thick brow furrowed. The sweet scent of incense was overwhelming, and, as I glanced towards the window by his desk, I could see the heap of ashes piling up underneath the burning sticks. I scrunched my nose, and continued forward until he turned at the sound of my footsteps. "Good, it is you. Come in."

"You wanted to see me?"

"Yes," he replied, glancing up with a smile and readjusting his uneven glasses. "I just wanted a quick word."

I approached his desk as he continued sorting, trying to smile back at him, though there was a sense of unease inside me. I couldn't think of any reason why he would need to speak to me outside of class time, good or bad.

I stopped by one of the smaller desks, sighing heavily when his gaze turned back to his precious books. He continued stacking them on the shelves, carefully holding together the fragile bindings and lose pages, and for a moment I was beginning to think he'd forgotten I was even there.

"Is something wrong?" I asked, after clearing my throat loudly enough for him to hear.

"No. It is nothing serious, Taryn. I am just a little concerned…about Nhanni."

I nodded in understanding, my eyes turning to the small crystal sphere at the corner of his desk. Sparks of coloured magic began flickering inside it, but Adriyel didn't take any notice of it and continued stacking books the same way a king stacks his gold. "I overheard those two boys this morning and I cannot help but worry about her," he explained as he worked. "I have been her mentor a long time; she has been here since she was just a child. I know that, as a teacher, I am not supposed to pick favourites, but I think of her almost…like a daughter."

"I know, Adriyel. It's completely understandable that you feel this way. Nhanni has had it rough her entire life and there's been no one but us to take care of her."

The crystal caught my attention again, as the colours began swirling like a vortex in the center. Something about it drew me in, like the crystal itself was calling me and beckoning for me to look.

Adriyel followed my gaze, and turned back toward me with a confused expression. Rather than asking what I'd been looking at, he continued. "It pains me that no one else seems to realize how powerful her magic actually is.

She passed the challenge today despite the fact that she cannot use words of power. It is *incredible*. Not only have the other students not realized it yet, but neither has Nhanni."

Adriyel's smile spread as he placed the final stacks of books back on the shelf. "It is almost worse because of that. The intensity of her magic astounded me, but despite how much she has improved, students at this school continue to judge and neglect her. All of this because of something she has no power over."

I nodded in agreement, sighing loudly and letting my shoulders fall. "And as they hurt her and her self-esteem lowers, her magic is weakened. If Nhanni only had confidence in herself she would be extremely powerful."

"More powerful than even *you*, perhaps," Adriyel added, his tone flattering.

Both our gazes turned to the crystal once again as the light exploded in a white flash. I jumped in surprise. Adriyel came around his desk quickly, and knelt beside the sphere as it began flashing colours and distorted images. I caught only a glimpse of a flickering violet fire, a deep green eye, long, slender fingers, and an emerald ring.

"Adriyel, what is that?" I asked after a moment, and shifted uncomfortably from foot to foot.

He stood and met my gaze, his smile returning, but there was something different in his eyes. I couldn't determine the right word for it at first, but I got a sense of worry from him, almost fear. "Nothing that should concern you, Taryn."

I kept his gaze for a long silence, unable to hide my sense that he was more concerned than he let on. I knew there was something he was hiding from me, I just didn't know his reasons for hiding it.

"I am glad you feel the same, Taryn," Adriyel continued, turning away from me. "With Jael's so-called 'friends' targeting her, and his training keeping me so busy...I was hoping you could keep an eye on her for me."

He glanced at me after a moment with a soft chuckle. "Not that I have to ask."

I grinned. "You're right. I don't have to be told. Looking out for her is all I've done since the first day I met her. Since we were too young to even understand the kind of danger that she's in."

"Thank you, Taryn. Nhannni is very lucky to have you as a friend."

After another strange silence, he cleared his throat, risking a quick glance toward the crystal sphere. "I am sorry to make you leave, Taryn. But there is still much work to be done before our next class. You should go find Nhanni."

"I understand. I will."

I returned his smile as best I could and turned back toward the door, my footsteps echoing loudly on the tile floor of the ballroom. I breathed a sigh of relief when I made it outside. I was about to continue down the stairwell when something stopped me.

That strange feeling had returned; that feeling like there was something connecting me to the crystal, constantly prodding at the back of my mind, trying to pull me close to it. I stood just outside the door, listening intently to the sound of Adriyel's movements across the room.

"Her voice…" I heard him whisper, the sound echoing so that it reached my ears. It was as if he was speaking to someone, thought the room had been empty moments ago. "*Where* is it hidden?"

Chapter seven

Nhanni

I was drowning, sinking in endless clear water, fighting to break the surface. My head pushed up, only long enough for me to catch a breath. I waved my arms back and forth uselessly, but there was a current pulling me wherever it went.

And it was going down.

I continued to sink, and I squinted through the water, looking for anything to pull myself up, hoping desperately for a miracle.

A figure broke the surface. I could make out little more than a shadow, diving towards me.

Too soon the last of my breath escaped my tight chest in tiny bubbles. My eyes began to close.

I gasped, my eyes shooting open to the familiar setting of my room, then I groaned.

A dream. Another *stupid* dream.

I rolled my head to the side, and saw from the light streaming through the window that the wake-up bell was going to sound in a few minutes.

I grabbed my journal and quickly wrote about the dream, as Adriyel asked me to, knowing I would likely forget it if I didn't.

I finished getting ready by the time the second bell rang, and got halfway to the ballroom before I realized what day it was.

Great...I thought to myself. What a day to begin sparring classes.

I was the last one to arrive at the ballroom, besides Taryn and Adriyel. The rest of the class was chatting away excitedly as usual. I approached my desk with a heavy sigh, and my mouth dropped open when I saw there was a bouquet of daisies on top.

Daisies...my favourite. Who would know that?

I noticed a card as well, but before I could read it, two strong arms grabbed me around the waist.

TARYN! I screamed in my head, and he laughed as he lifted me and spun me around. Put me down! What's going on?!

He set me back on my feet, smiling even more than usual. "What do you mean 'what's going on?'," he replied, pushing a box into my hands and kissing my cheek. "Happy birthday."

My face turned hot. He'd never done that before.

I glanced at the box he'd placed in my hands, and froze when I realized it was a jewelry box of blue velvet. With a sideways glance at Taryn I opened it slowly, my eyes widening.

I grabbed his hand automatically. Taryn...

"They match the ring I got you. Do you like them?"

I looked back up from the earrings, giving him a disapproving glance. Most of the time I tried to *forget* how much money his family had, and he knew it very well.

"Relax…they weren't *very* expensive."

I tried, and failed, to collect my thoughts. Wasn't *one* expensive ring enough? I have eyes, Taryn. Knowing you, they're priceless antiques.

"I promise they're not."

And the ring?

His face turned red and I sighed loudly. Oh no…it *is* a priceless antique.

He looked embarrassed at first, then laughed when he saw my expression. "It's okay, Nhanni. I wanted to."

You shouldn't keep getting me gifts. I don't need them.

"It's only fair. You get *me* a gift every year too. Please wear them."

I sighed loudly. Fine.

His bright smile returned as I put on the earrings, set with sparkling clear gems that matched my favourite ring. It was the ring Taryn gave me my first birthday after we met.

His smile spread. "I knew it! They're perfect."

I sighed again in disapproval, and threw my arms around him.

Thank you, I love them.

When he released me, I turned back and grabbed the card off my desk. Taryn noticed the flowers, and froze. "Who are those from?"

The card read :

To my favourite student (do not tell anyone else I said that). I am so proud of all you have accomplished this year.

Happy birthday.

Adriyel

He remembered.

I smiled and handed the card to Taryn, who relaxed instantly as he read it.

"So much for not favouring any student," he muttered, returning my smile as he sat. "Great! He knows what you're favourite flowers are too! That's hard to compete with…"

I rolled my eyes and gestured to the shiny earrings. He grinned just as Adriyel and Eldyn strode through the doors, followed by a handful of excited students. There were fewer than forty people in the entire academy, which was why I recognised almost all of the students in Eldyn's class. It was also why we each got our own rooms, which I appreciated.

The sound of chatter throughout the ballroom was doubled now, and Adriyel quickly raised his hands and motioned for us to be silent. "Good morning class. We are ready to begin your training just as soon as we go over the rules." Adriyel went over to his desk.

Eldyn nodded. "It is simple. We will begin with one-on-one matches, where you may only use attack and defense spells against each other. Adriyel and I will be supervising in case any of you tries something else. If all of you are responsible about this and nothing goes wrong, we will improve these rules in the following classes."

Adriyel looked over the group of students. "Everyone understand?"

He received unenthusiastic 'yeah's from across the room, and he nodded in approval. "Alright. Everyone please come to the center and form a circle around those tiles. Do not cross them; those are our boundaries."

We quickly created the circle and, miraculously, remained silent after we finished. Eldyn paced around the inside of the boundary, eyeing each student as he passed them as if trying to sense which one of us was the most frightened. "Would anyone like to go first?"

Taryn squeezed my hand and smiled. "I will."

"Wonderful. Thank you, Taryn," Eldyn said excitedly as Taryn made his way into the center of the circle. "Any challengers?"

The room was abruptly silent.

After a moment, Adriyel laughed outrageously, stepping forward. "No one dares challenge the great Taryn? Either one of you volunteers or *I* chose."

None of us were willing to speak or raise a hand, and Adriyel grinned. "Alright then. Come on up, Kyndra."

A girl from Eldyn's class sighed heavily, her expression slightly worried as she entered the circle as well.

"Begin on my signal," Adriyel instructed, when Eldyn turned and joined the crowd. "Ready?" he asked. It was probably his favourite word.

Taryn and Kyndra both raised their hands.

"Go!"

Taryn, not wasting any time, instantly threw an attack spell at her. "*Incurro!*"

Then another.

And another.

Kyndra looked absolutely terrified, shouting "*Contego!*" as she blocked his attacks and stumbled away from him. She managed to attack once and spin out of the way, as Taryn sidestepped and attacked again. Kyndra raised her hands to her side in the middle of her spin, towards Taryn. "*Incurro!*"

The students shrieked and bent low as the attack flew over their heads, and Kyndra stood stunned. Taryn had moved in an instant, and was now standing behind her.

"*Incurro!*"

As the spell flew towards her, the red glow of Adriyel's magic appeared and she slid across the floor, unharmed.

Taryn relaxed his stance, grinning to himself.

"Well done, Taryn!" Adriyel congratulated him, re-entering the circle. "And well done, Kyndra. Nice try."

Taryn helped Kyndra to her feet, and told her something I couldn't hear, before returning to my side and taking my hand again. Kyndra, bewitched by his smile, turned and watched him as she walked back to her spot.

That was quick...I noted.

He grinned even more. "Piece of cake."

"Who will be next? Let's see…" Eldyn said to himself, looking over the crowd as the students began shifting nervously under his gaze. I noticed he was glancing towards the two guys Adriyel had dragged out of class the day before; Morahn and Gabe.

"Morahn, how about you?" Eldyn asked.

He nodded, and reluctantly made his way towards the circle as Eldyn glanced in my direction. "And Nhanni."

Taryn squeezed my hand tightly at the same time Adriyel's eyes widened. "Eldyn, that is *not* a good idea-"

"Nhanni must learn to defend herself like the other students, Adriyel. She will be completely fine with both of us watching."

Adriyel sighed loudly, before waving me forward. "Come on up, Nhanni."

I met Taryn's gaze as he shook his head, and slowly moved towards the circle with small, hesitant steps. Adriyel noticed that Taryn hadn't released my hand, and came forward. "She will be fine, Taryn."

I nodded to him and he finally released me, but stayed on the edge of the circle. His intense eyes watched Morahn like a hawk, as we raised our hands and took our stances.

I breathed deeply, staring forward.

"Go!" shouted Adriyel.

At first, nothing happened. Morahn seemed to realize I wouldn't attack and shoved his hands forward. "*Incurro!*"

I tried to summon the defence spell, which failed, and I quickly dove out of the way as Morahn's spell sped past me.
Taryn's foot had inched forward and Adriyel put a restraining hand on his shoulder. Every student had gone silent, and they were all watching intently, holding their breaths.

I dove when Morahn attacked again, and raised my hand as I stumbled forward, sending an attack spell in his direction. Blue light seemed to explode inside the circle, and both of us were forced backward.

"*Contego!*" To my disappointment Morahn blocked the attack, and I hastily threw the spell at him again and again. He blocked every one, never losing focus, and I let my hands fall when I began to feel weak.

Morahn saw his chance. "*Incurro!*"

My eyes widened. The spell sped toward me, sending me flying back, but Morahn didn't back down. Teachers and students were shouting, their hands waving and motioning for him to stop,

"*Contego!*" someone shouted. Green light flashed brightly before me, and Morahn and I were forced to shield our eyes.

Jael ran into the circle. "*Impedo!*"

Light spun like a flying boomerang, wrapping itself around Morahn, who stood frozen in shock. The spell became iron chains around him, producing mixed reactions from the watching teachers and students.

"*What*?!" Morahn gasped in surprise, before losing balance and falling over.

I was still sprawled across the floor, my eyes wide, as Jael came towards me. I sat up, and heat rose to my cheeks when he supported me with one arm around my waist. His hand touched my cheek. "Are you hurt?'

"A *trapping spell*, Jael?" Adriyel said in disbelief as he approached. "That is an extremely advanced spell! How do you know it?"

"Do we really have to talk about this *now*? Nhanni was hit with that attack!"

Taryn came running, and he and Adriyel knelt beside me as well. "Are you alright, Nhanni?" Taryn asked worriedly, reaching for my hand.

I shook my head. I don't think it actually hit me, for some reason. I feel fine.

"Well?" Adriyel asked impatiently as Taryn breathed a sigh of relief.

"She's fine," Taryn repeated to them, then glanced at Adriyel. "We're lucky. Morahn's spell wasn't that strong, and it didn't harm her."

"You had better take her to our healer, just in case," Adriyel replied.

Taryn nodded, and he and Jael slowly helped me to my feet. I put my arm around Taryn's shoulder and leaned against him when I almost fell over.

"I'll come," Jael said suddenly, as Taryn led me towards the doors.

"No!" Adriyel shouted, so loudly that I flinched at the sound. We all froze in shock; students and teachers all staring at him with wide eyes.

Adriyel sighed. "No..." he said more calmly, but grasped Jael's arm with a firm grip. "I think it would be best if you do not go with them." His eyes fell on me. "You have done enough."

Chapter eight

Taryn

I was just leaving Nhanni's room, closing the door quietly behind me, when I heard him slowly approaching from down the corridor. I knew it was him, even before I turned at the sound of his heavy footsteps; even before I saw the embarrassed look on his face, as if I'd caught him sneaking out of his room after hours.

I rolled my eyes to myself and turned to face him, crossing my arms. "It's late, Jael."

"I know," he replied, walking up almost shyly, with his hands shoved in his pockets. "Adriyel wouldn't let me out of his sight all day."

I sighed. "You know…there's a reason for that."

He shrugged to show he didn't understand, and when neither of us spoke for some time, he cleared his throat nervously. "I just came to make sure Nhanni's okay."

"I know," I replied, and planted my feet solidly in front of her door when he tried to glance past me. "*That*'s the reason."

After a short silence, he released a long breath, his eyes falling. It was then I knew that Adriyel had spoken with Jael about this already, but that he'd come looking for Nhanni despite Adriyel's warnings. "Is she okay?"

"The healer said that she's fine, and just asked me to stay with her until she fell asleep. Even so, Adriyel doesn't want her sparring for a while."

Jael nodded to himself, looking relieved at first. Soon though, his expression became a mixture between anger and sadness. "So that's it then? Adriyel is going to do his best to keep her away from me now? And all because of-"

"He can see what's going on," I interrupted, taking a step towards him. We stood the same height; eye to eye. "And so can I."

His expression hardened as I said this, and we stayed frozen like statues while the minutes passed long. Jael's eyes were like piercing shears of green ice, but I held my ground, unable to do anything else but keep my eyes on his as we waited for each other to speak.

Finally, when I decided he wouldn't be the first to break the silence, I glanced towards the door. "Stay away from Nhanni."

There was another pause. When I glanced back at him, I was surprised that his face had fallen, and the sadness in his eyes was so real that I almost moved aside to let him pass. "You and Adriyel won't even let me see her?"

"Well there's not much we can do, considering Nhanni has to continue her training and Adriyel happens to be her mentor too. But if anything like that happens again-" I began, looking him straight in the eye. "I'm sure he'll figure something out."

I started to get annoyed when he still didn't move, eyeing the closed door for what seemed like an eternity.

Nhanni and I were the only ones with a key to her room. What was he going to do? Pick the lock?

Jael seemed to read my expression, and sighed in defeat. I relaxed my tense position, but remained standing where I was.
"She's my friend. I just…I just wanted to see her and make sure she was okay."

I shook my head as I finally strode past him, chuckling quietly to myself. "I can tell you're lying.

Book two

Chapter nine

Nhanni

The thundering bells were slowly dying, and hushed voices were rising into the light of his vision. Of all the people at this academy, the only one who could hear the silent voice was the one who relied most on what he heard.

The one person who, for so long, had been blinded and tricked by what was right in front of him now saw me in the background, nothing more than a small hesitant whisper, and left everything he knew to follow me there.

Lives come together, flowing eternally like blended watercolours, an image formed so miraculously from a blank void that its beauty cannot be imitated or remade.

Lives come together, woven and connected like a spider's web of unbreakable silver thread. There is no end to this chain that binds us, no end to our paintings of masterpieces and writings of miracles.

There will always be life, flowing, blending, and growing out. Life lives here, under the sky, with roots desperately grasping soil and branches longingly reaching up to the stars. Life lives here, in a silence and stillness from our circling galaxy. In small tableau moments that mark a small instant of a lifetime, but an instant of connection.

A pause.

The world only grows louder in silence, when the hidden whispers finally come to us...heard. When the soft song, long forgotten, is finally remembered. There is room for stillness in those instants, only room for a dome of everlasting blue...blurring out of focus as a slowly drifting speck of dust catches the eye.

I sighed heavily to myself, and closed my journal before I could write any more. I was still completely shocked and confused by what had happened the day before. It wasn't like I'd been in any real danger; Adriyel and Eldyn had both been there, and Morahn's spell hadn't been strong enough to do me any harm.

I didn't want to be ungrateful, but why had Jael interfered? Even though over the past month our partnership had grown into a real friendship, the way he was acting was strange.

Adriyel had told me earlier to stay in my room for at least today, but I hadn't realised how quickly time had passed. Classes were now over. Jael and his friends would be by the lake.

I sighed again and put down my journal. *You need to go talk to him.*

I came out the door right by the lake not long after, and glanced around to make sure there were no professors or coaches before approaching. Jael was easy to spot, watching with a bright smile on his face as the others dove into the deep water. His hair hung in wet strands, and small droplets of water were still clinging to his face. I hesitated when I saw that he was surrounded by most of his friends, but took a deep breath and continued forward.

Several boys noticed me, and all grinned while they tried to get Jael's attention.

"Hey, look who it is!" one of them said.

Almost everyone laughed as Jael jumped to his feet. "Nhanni?"

"What is *she* doing here?" Gabe said in surprise, stepping forward.

Jael pushed him aside and came up to me, taking my arm and leading me away from the rest of them. "If Adriyel sees you here-"

I'm sorry to barge in, I said, then folded my arms over my chest. *But you have some explaining to do.*

He sighed. "I wish everyone would just-!" he began, his anger surprising me. "First Adriyel, then the guys, then Taryn, and now-!"

Taryn?!

Jael stopped abruptly when my eyes grew wide.

You spoke with Taryn?

"Sort of…" he replied, running his hand threw his dripping hair and refusing to meet my gaze. "It wasn't a particularly long conversation."

I shook my head. Taryn must have confronted him; I should have known. *What did he say?*

"What *everyone* has been saying!"

We were silent a moment, and I cocked my eyebrow to show that I didn't know what he was talking about.

Jael sighed again, not seeming to want to reply. "He told me…to stay away from you."

"What is taking so long, Jael?" one of his friends groaned, making everyone else glance in our direction.

"Forget her, Jael," someone else said. "You can talk training later. You don't have to be nice just because she's your partner."

Jael whirled around. "Give me a minute!"

I hadn't expected him to stand up for me again, but my face hardened as he turned back.

"Look Nhanni, I'm sorry. But I don't understand why you, and everyone else, are making such a big deal out of this. You were in trouble and I stepped in to help. You're just my partner."

Clearly.

"I didn't mean-" he said in surprise, his shoulders falling. "I meant that I'm just looking out for you. Last time I checked, that's what friends do for each other."

Am I really your friend, Jael?! I demanded, getting frustrated now. *Because I'm starting to think Taryn's right and your stupid pride is all you care about!*

I turned to leave.

"Nhanni wait!"

"Yeah, come back!" came Gabe's voice.

I turned in surprise, and saw Jael pushing him away. "Alright, Gabe."

"No, I'm serious. Why doesn't she stay? I mean, now that you guys are so close."

"Knock it off."

Gabe was approaching me, and I took a step back. "It's okay, Nhanni," he said, grinning hugely and gesturing to the rest of the guys. "Why don't you join us?"

He grasped my hand. As I tried uselessly to free myself, he only laughed and tightened his grip. "What's the matter? Scared of a little *water*?"

My eyes widened. *Water?* I shook my head furiously, still unable to pull away. *Please stop!* I screamed in my thoughts. *You don't understand-*

"Let her go, Gabe!" Jael was trying to reach me, but Gabe kept pushing him back.

"Come on, Nhanni!" Gabe said, locking his arms around my waist and lifting me as easily as if I were a doll. "Join us for a swim!"

"*Gabe!*"

I only had time to take one deep breath before I was thrown into the lake. I would have screamed, but I quickly clamped my mouth shut as the water surrounded me. I tried to push myself up to take another breath, but the weight of my uniform pulled me deeper.

After a while my chest began to tighten.

I was drowning, sinking in endless clear water, fighting to break the surface. My head pushed up, only long enough for me to catch a breath. I waved my arms back and forth uselessly, but there was a current pulling me wherever it went.

And it was going *down*.

I continued to sink and squinted through the water, looking for anything to pull myself up, hoping desperately for a miracle.

A figure broke the surface. I could make out little more than a shadow, diving towards me in seconds. Too soon, the last of my breath escaped my tight chest in tiny bubbles.

My eyes began to close.

Two arms cradled me, and I could only hope desperately that it was Jael, and he had realized what was happening. The moment my head was above the water, I took a huge breath and began to gasp, my nails digging into my rescuer's arm.

"You're okay, Nhanni. Breathe," he repeated as he carried me back to land.

It wasn't Jael. *Thank you,* was all I could say as he gently set me down. *Thank you, Taryn.*

He nodded before springing to his feet, stalking angrily towards Gabe. "Are you *insane*?"

"Relax, Taryn. It was just a joke."

I gasped when Taryn grabbed a fistful of Gabe's shirt, shoving him roughly against a tree. "She's terrified of the water, you *idiot*! She can't swim!"

It was Gabe who looked terrified. "I didn't know!"

"Maybe next time you should check before throwing her into the deep end of a lake!" Taryn shoved him again before dropping him and kneeling beside me. He pulled my arm over his shoulder and slowly helped me to my feet.

Jael looked just as furious. "Why didn't you stop, Gabe?"

"I didn't-"

"You could have *killed* her!"

"What is going *on* here?!"

Instantly, we all froze, and turned to see Adriyel approaching from the door close by.

Oh great... I thought to myself.

Adriyel stopped, noticing me and Taryn in our soaked uniforms.

"Gabe," Taryn replied through clenched teeth. "Gabe threw Nhanni in the water."

"What? Don't you know she can't swim?"

Gabe's eyes fell on me. He actually looked sorry. "*Now* I do."

Adriyel grabbed his arm. "You will come with me to see the head professor. Taryn, you take her back to the healer please."

Taryn nodded, putting his arm around me and slowly leading me away from the lake.

Adriyel's eyes fell on Jael. "And *you*...I thought you understood that-"

"You can blame *me*, Adriyel," Taryn said, glaring at Jael as we passed him. "Apparently I didn't make myself clear enough the first time."

There was a long silence. The rest of the guys were glancing back and forth between us in confusion, not seeming to have a clue what was going on. I felt bad when I saw Jael's face fall. Taryn and Adriyel were placing the blame on *him*, but *I* was the one who had come here.

I was about to tell Taryn that it was *my* fault, but Jael spoke first. "I do understand, Adriyel, and I know that I am to blame."

My breath caught, and a sound like a surprised squeak escaped my lips.

"The reason I wanted to talk to Nhanni was to ask her if she needed my help. After what happened in sparring class, I thought I could help her with some spells."

Taryn and Adriyel exchanged a glance. I kept my eyes on Jael, who stubbornly refused to meet my gaze.

He lied. I didn't know whether to feel thankful or furious right now.

Adriyel turned to Jael, and actually smiled. "That's not a bad idea, Jael."

Taryn and I both glanced at him in surprise.

"Indeed, it would really help her, and you are definitely more than capable. I think you are the perfect person for the job," Adriyel continued, and I noticed a not-so-subtle hint of warning in his voice. "You are *friends*, after all."

Tell him no.

Taryn glanced at me. "Nhanni?"

Jael glanced at me worriedly, and Adriyel whirled around to face us.

"What is she saying?" he asked, taking a step forward.

"She doesn't want to train with Jael."

I glared in Jael's direction while everyone else glanced at me in surprise. Jael looked hurt as his eyes met mine, but I turned my face away. *Get me away from him, Taryn.*

Taryn seemed surprised by my anger, but nodded and led me toward the doors of The Academy. Everyone's eyes followed us, but they remained silent till we reached the entrance.

"Nhanni…" Jael said sadly.

I slammed the door behind us.

Chapter ten

Frustrations

-Feeling alone
-Not being able to say what is meant to be said
-Anger clouding my mind, like an eclipse swallows the sun
-When a midnight chills passes over me. I can't sleep; there is too much to think about
-Not being able to say it out loud; to say what I wish. To do what I dream
-Feeling trapped, not on the inside but on the outside. And all I want to do is peer in

It isn't chains holding me back, but a string.
A string holding me down.
So easily broken.
But too guiltily ridden of.

I heard the doorknob rattle, and closed my journal as Taryn came in, smiling brightly. "All packed?"

I nodded in response, and he grabbed my bag off the floor. "Alright. Let's go!" He held the door open for me and took my hand as we made our way down the hall.

It was getting warmer outside with the coming of spring, which made it the perfect time for a break. I was excited to spend time at Taryn's home, the home he'd inherited once he turned eighteen. His parents had died before I'd even met him, but he rarely talked about it, so that was the extent of what I knew. The huge house was far from The Academy, so we hadn't been there since Christmas.

I was also glad to be getting away from school and training for a change; to relax and spend time at the only other place I considered my home.

We stepped through the huge doors, and I shielded my eyes against the bright sun burning above us. The light outside was uncomfortably harsh in comparison to the dimly lit halls of The Academy.

Taryn tensed, and I noticed him glaring toward the benches, where Jael and his friends were sitting. Jael was watching us, and looked like he was about to come talk to us, but we reached the small carriage that was waiting.

"Iceglade, please," Taryn muttered to the coachman, then opened the door and shoved me in. He continued to glare at them even after I was inside. I flashed him a look as he slid in next to me, but he didn't meet my gaze.

I took his hand. *Will you relax for a second? The point of the long weekend is for us to get away from all this. We can forget about magic, and Jael, for the next couple of days.*

He sighed in response, turning to face me. "I know. I'm sorry I act this way."

It's okay, I'm glad you do, I replied with a smile. *You're always looking out for me.*

"And I'm glad you haven't spoken with Jael since the lake incident," he added as the carriage jostled and began to move. "But to be honest, I'd rather you concentrated on avoiding *Gabe*."

I couldn't hide my surprise at this. *Really?*

"Of course. Gabe's the one who tried to *drown* you."

He didn't try to-

"I know, I know," Taryn replied, rolling his eyes at me. "Still, Gabe's a bad person. At least with Jael you aren't in any danger. He's kind of...protective of you."

Don't worry, Taryn. There's no way I'll go anywhere near him again.

He sighed in relief, before glancing back at me with a small smile. "When you say that do you mean Gabe...or Jael?"

I turned away, staring out the window in case my expression was revealing how truly angry I was. Both.

We were silent until we reached the main road, and Taryn seemed eager to get my mind off of Jael. "We have a long journey ahead of us."

I grinned and pulled out a novel thicker than my fist. I'd always brought books on long rides to pass the time, even though I spent a lot of time watching the landscape change through the small window. I always loved traveling to far-away places, but I never got to travel very often. The furthest I'd ever been was when Taryn brought me to the city, where we'd caught our first glimpses of the palace's tall towers.

I tried to read for the first few minutes of the ride, but I was too distracted; my mind was wandering throughout the journey and I was already tired before it was even dark outside. Taryn didn't look tired at all. When he noticed my eyelids falling, he grinned and reached for my hand. "We're still a few hours away. Why don't you get some sleep?"

I nodded and squeezed his hand tightly. Don't let the coachman keep going if he gets tired.

"I won't."

I sat back against the soft seat and sighed, letting my drooping eyelids close.

What felt like moments later, my eyes opened slightly. I could barely see through my long eyelashes and the flashes of light. The carriage was still jostling lightly, the wheels passing over stones and dipping into holes in the road. It was dark outside and streams of moonlight were flashing through the window as we passed behind trees and houses.

I realized that my head now rested on Taryn's shoulder. He had his arm around me, and was staring out the side window, unaware that I was awake. Normally I would be embarrassed, but I just sighed, too tired to care.

My eyes began to close again, and I heard Taryn's faint chuckle. "Go back to sleep, Nhanni. I'll wake you when we get there."

I stared out at the rows of people, gripping the staff tightly in my hand. Their smiling faces were lit by the streams of light, pouring through windows as tall as the room itself. All of them had their eyes on me, as if they were all waiting for me to do something. Anything.

From the front row, Jael nodded to me, his eyes sparkling and a smile pulling at the corners of his mouth. I smiled back and stood tall, taking a deep breath.

Once more I looked over the crowd, then raised the staff of gold above my head.

"Nhanni?"

I woke again to Taryn's voice. I noticed the carriage had finally stopped.

Taryn still had his arm around me, and was shaking me gently. "Nhanni, wake up. I have a surprise for you."

I shivered and blinked. Taryn laughed lightly, cocking his head toward the open door where the cool breeze was coming from. "*Look.*"

My tired eyes could barely make out the familiar face grinning at me from outside.

All of a sudden, I was wide awake.

My eyes widened. Dad?

Chapter eleven

Adriyel

I sighed in relief when Taryn finally opened the door to his house, shaking my rain-soaked hair away from my eyes. "It's about time."

Nhanni's father, Rowyn, appeared from around the corner. "Good, you've arrived. We were surprised to get your message, Adriyel."

I shivered and quickly kicked off my boots, hanging my dripping cloak by the door. "Sorry I am late. I had to stop the carriage when it started raining so hard the coachmen could barely see. It did not help that it is pitch black outside."

I stepped into the huge house and Rowyn and I shook hands. "It has been a long time, Rowyn."

He nodded in agreement and we all took a seat in the living room, sighing in unison. I glanced nervously towards the hallway, and listened intently for any sound that would alert me if Nhanni had awoken.

"So let me see if I understand correctly…" Rowyn began, clasping his hands in front of him. "You are thinking about sending Nhanni back home with me?"

When Taryn nodded, I cleared my throat before speaking. "We have not decided if we should pull her out of The Academy yet; that is why we are all here. Taryn and I thought it would be best to discuss this before making a decision."

"I'm still confused," Rowyn put in. "No one's told me *why* we're even considering this yet. What is it Nhanni's done exactly? You've never once had to talk to me about her schooling before, and you certainly wouldn't request to see me face to face if the matter was not important."

"It's nothing *Nhanni* has done," Taryn explained, rubbing his hands together as he stared at the floor.

I recognized the look in his eyes: the sense of worry for Nhanni's well being, the longing to comfort her and speak the truth about things she no longer understood, the guilt that we were speaking behind her back in the first place.

I shook my head. "Our concern is Jael, the apprentice whom the Oracle predicted would take my place as royal sorcerer. I am sure you are still familiar with the prophecy?"

"Yes, I know about it. But what does this boy have to do with Nhanni?"

Taryn and I exchanged another glance, neither of us wanting to explain.

After a long silence, Rowyn froze, a look of shock overtaking his expression."Wait one moment…" he said softly as his eyes widened. "Adriyel, are you telling me that-"

"I am afraid it is exactly what you think, Rowyn. Exactly what I feared would happen," I said calmly. "We have noticed that the boy has developed…feelings towards Nhanni. It appears they are no more than friends right now, but I am worried it might become more if he continues to see her."

"I'm beginning to think he feels that way already, Adriyel." Taryn added quietly.

Rowyn shook his head. "She must come home with me, Adriyel, you know this. I can't allow anything more to happen; I can't have any of Jael's enemies threatening her. Her voice was stolen when we realized her incredible power as a *child*. She is vulnerable enough as it is."

"We know, Rowyn," I said, pushing myself to my feet with a soft sigh. I could not stop myself from pacing across the floor the way I always did when I was anxious. "We know that this places her in danger already. That is why this decision is a difficult one to make. She is too vulnerable to be allowed anywhere *near* Jael, but she will remain vulnerable for the rest of her life unless she completes her training with me. Or, unless the Royal Army and I are finally able to recover her voice."

Taryn glanced at me suddenly, a strange expression on his face. "The crystal…"

I tensed as he said this. I could assume by his distant expression that he was remembering the images he had seen in my glass crystal some time ago, small glimpses into what I had hoped was the location of Nhanni's stolen voice. Luckily, Rowan continued speaking before Taryn had the chance to pester me for an explanation.

"Of course," Rowyn said, his eyes falling on me as I continued to pace nervously around the room. "Has it shown you anything?"

"Nothing. I am afraid Raveena has hidden it very well; so well that even I cannot see it."

I did not stop pacing, even after Taryn cast me an annoyed glance, and Rowyn sighed heavily. "I'm afraid you may be right then, Adriyel. We can't pull Nhanni out of school so near the end of her apprenticeship. Besides, we may be jumping to conclusions about the boy's feelings towards her."

We were all silent a moment.

I glanced at Taryn."What is your opinion, Taryn? I believe you should have a say; you have been her best friend nearly her entire life. It would be upsetting for the both of you if Nhanni was to return home to Windylow."

His head hung. "I wasn't going to bring it up, but it's true. Of course I would rather she stayed at The Academy. We've been there together for over twelve years. Nhanni did not seem pleased with Jael when we left, and I would be there to make sure he keeps his distance."

Rowyn had his head in his hands, nodding to himself. "I think it may be the best thing for us to do, right now," he finally said. "Nhanni's training should be our top priority. She was a prodigy before her voice was stolen, after all, and despite all that's happened, her magic is still with her. And you said she is able to summon her magic at will, without the use of words of power. Some sorcerers will definitely still be threatened by her, perhaps even Raveena herself. We can't allow *anyone*, especially Ravenna, to harm her again."

I nodded in agreement. "I think it is decided, then. Nhanni will continue her training at The Academy with me."

I glanced at Taryn. "And you will keep an eye on her, as always. Once the full extent of her magic is realized, she will be even more powerful than *you*, Taryn, and perhaps even *me*. With such power she will not be vulnerable. It is the best solution, for the time being."

"I hope you are right. I hope Jael only thinks of Nhanni as a friend," Taryn said with another sigh, staring at the floor.

"I hope so too, " I told him, grinning hugely as I met Rowyn's gaze. "You have enough competition for her already."

His eyes bulged, and Rowyn and I laughed.

Taryn 'humph'ed and looked away, but glanced at me out of the corner of his eyes. "What competition?'

"Oh nothing…I just noticed a young man watching her at lunch this one time. You had better get a move on, my boy."

He 'humph'ed again, standing and quickly exiting down the hall. "Whatever. I don't think of her that way."

Rowyn and I laughed even harder, shaking our heads at his attempt to appear as if he didn't care.

"I am no fool, Taryn," I called after him. "I can tell you are lying."

Chapter twelve

Nhanni

I woke to the scent of fresh bread and pastries. Immediately, I leapt to my feet and pulled my gown over my head. I could recognise my father's home cooking anywhere; he used to make me flat bread with sweet syrup and strawberries for breakfast, even if it wasn't a special occasion. I hurried down the hall and found Taryn already awake. He was seated at the table, watching my father work with quiet interest.

It was because of my father's skills that he no longer lived in Arheynia. My aunt, who was also a wonderful baker, asked him to return to Windylow and help her run her own bakery in the city. My father and his sister were two of the few sorcerers able to conjure charms into their baked goods. Often, when I was young, he would bake healing spells into small cakes if I ever got ill, or sleeping spells into my dinner on the nights I refused to go to sleep.

I couldn't help but smile at the look of wonder of Taryn's face as he watched. When I came into the kitchen, his wide smile grew even wider, and he motioned for me to take the seat next to him. "It's been so long since Rowyn made us breakfast. I'd almost forgotten how masterfully he mixes spells into his bread and cakes."

Father turned and mirrored Taryn's smile, and I tried not to laugh at the sight of flour sprinkled over his freckled cheeks and nose.

"Morning!" he said cheerfully, kissing me lightly on the cheek. "I'm making your favourite."

I know. I could smell your flat bread from all the way down the hall. I miss waking up to that scent.

Taryn nodded, picking up on the hint of unhappiness in my tone of voice. He always seemed to know that I missed my father more than I usually let on. Father placed two full plates in front of us, and sat across from us without cleaning his face or removing his apron.

"Is there any way you can stay longer, Rowyn? Nhanni and I don't have to be back for three more days," Taryn said while he gulped down his food.

"No. I'm afraid I must leave tomorrow, as planned. My sister will be expecting me, and I am already behind on several spells."

I exchanged a disappointed glance with Taryn, before following his example and eating my breakfast. Speaking of spells...which did you use in this flatbread we're eating?

"Oh, just a spell to relieve fatigue. Both of you looked absolutely exhausted when you arrived. I imagine your training has become harder now that you are in the last year of your apprenticeship."

It has. Thanks, dad.

He nodded while he ate, and after a moment a huge smile spread across his face. "I just remembered…I brought something back with me, from the palace of Windylow."

"You've been to the palace?" Taryn asked in astonishment.

"Yes, only once. Nhanni's aunt and I were sent for, several days before the princess' birthday. The king hoped we would prepare the cake for her banquet. It was one of our best works, I must say."

So, what did you bring us?

My father stood and removed his apron, but ignored the flour still sticking to his face. "Follow me to my carriage, and I will show you."

Taryn and I both abandoned our half-eaten breakfast and followed him out into the pleasantly warm weather. He led us around to the stables, where both our carriages had been moved after we arrived. The horses rested in clean stalls nearby.

Father jumped onto the steps and reached to the roof of his carriage. He grunted as he tried to undo heavy leather straps, and after a moment motioned towards Taryn. "Give me a hand, would you Taryn? These straps are stubborn, and this thing is quite heavy. Took us ages just to get it on there in the first place"

"Sure." Taryn jumped onto the steps on the other side to help him, and I began loosening more of the straps. "Rowyn…is this what I think it is?"

"Indeed. Alright, bring it down."

Taryn grunted and pushed the huge, flat object from one side. My father supported the other as it slid from the roof.

It was a mirror, taller than my father.

It is absolutely beautiful! What's it for?

"It's called *Magia Speculum*," my father explained. "A looking glass. Sorcerers use it to speak over long distances, and some sorcerers even have the power to transport themselves to other places."

"It's wonderful, Rowyn," Taryn said with an ecstatic smile. "I know just where to put it. Will you help me bring it to the living room, the one with those windows on the West side? The lighting will be perfect in there."

Rowyn nodded, and I followed as they each lifted a side of the long mirror and hauled it through the door. When we made it into the right room and they gently set it down again, I saw that Taryn was right. There was a perfect place for it against an empty wall, where the sun would hit the surface just beautifully as it began to set in the evening.

Rowyn sighed with relief when he put the heavy-looking mirror down, and turned to me. "I am sorry that I must leave so soon. But this looking glass will allow you and Taryn to communicate with me anytime you return to his home. You will be able to see and hear anyone, no matter where they are, but you can only walk through the glass if the place you wish to go has another looking glass. That's why I have another mirror like this one back in Windylow."

Really? Oh, it's perfect! Now we can see you for Christmas and Thanksgiving. We can even talk when we have another long weekend! Thank you! I exclaimed, and father laughed as I jumped and threw my arms around him.

"It's very beautiful, Rowyn. You didn't have to go through the trouble."

"It's no trouble, I promise. The king offered it to my sister as part of our payment, and since she has one in our home already she suggested that I bring it here for you two. It's been even longer since either of you have seen *her*. Perhaps you can come through the glass to Windylow sometime."

Taryn laughed at the idea, shaking his head. "That is an advanced spell, Rowyn. Several spellbooks past the one we are learning from right now."

"Shouldn't be a problem for *you* then, should it?" Father teased, and squeezed my shoulders. "And from what I hear from Adriyel, you're doing marvellously as well, Nhanni."

I smiled brightly and turned to the mirror, hesitantly reaching to the surface. *How does it work? Do I just-*

The surface rippled suddenly, making me stop short. All three of us stared at the images taking shape in the glass. The melody of images were almost dreamlike, and for a long time I could make out nothing but flickering violet flames in a tall fireplace. Taryn and Rowyn gasped in unison as the mirror pulled into focus. It showed a tall woman, who was facing away from us and staring intently at the fire as it swayed and flickered before her. For a moment I felt her aura, a strong radiating energy that seemed to surround her like a cloud.

The woman in the mirror was still, as if sensing our presence as well, and turned and looked directly at me. I couldn't tell if the expression she wore was one of horror, or astonishment. Something clicked as our eyes met; it was like that moment when you can't remember someone by name until you see them face to face. Though I knew I'd never met this woman, I knew exactly who she was the very moment I saw her face. It was her vibrant green eyes. Like Jael's.

Taryn quickly grabbed me, and pulled me away from the mirror. I blinked as I was jerked from my trance-like state, and instantly the images in the mirror rippled and vanished once again. I staggered. Taryn reacted quickly, and supported me when he saw I was about to fall. "Nhanni…how did you-?"

I-I don't know. I just touched the glass and the image appeared...and it was like the mirror was trying to pull me in somehow.

"Just amazing...I've never seen you conjure such a difficult spell before. It was like you weren't even trying," My father said, staring with an expression torn between excitement and shock.

I was silent a long time, breathing deeply and trying to slow my heart. Was that...who I think it was?

Taryn met Rowyn's gaze, before nodding to me. "Yes. I'm afraid it was."

Chapter thirteen

Two days later

I watched the red sun slowly dip in the sky. My feet were dangling over the edge of the pond but I didn't dare go deeper, even though everyone had done their best to teach me how to swim. I couldn't stay above water for long, but at least I wasn't in as much danger of drowning.

I heard the door open, and turned to see Taryn coming outside. "You shouldn't be out here by yourself," he said as he came down the slope towards me.

I flashed an annoyed look at how overprotective he was, making him laugh. "I see…you've realized what day it is." He sat next to me by the edge of the pond, and took my hand.

We have to leave tomorrow, and going back to school is always hard after I come back here. I didn't even realize how much I missed my dad until I saw him. I wish Windylow wasn't so far away.

He nodded. "Yes, it has been a while. Windylow is so far that he couldn't even make it for your eighteenth birthday. But in a few months, school will be over. And won't be apprentices, but real sorcerers."

We sat in silence a while. Taryn watched me, his pale eyes intense, and I knew right away he was thinking the same thing I was. Neither of us wanted to be the first to say it.

Taryn didn't look away. After a moment, I finally took a breath and met his gaze. *What will happen when it's over? If we pass Adriyel's class and become sorcerers we will work for the king. We may never see my father except for once a year, and the king's army is so busy that even if we both make it we will probably rarely see each other.*

"I know. But it won't be as bad as you think. The Army has been busy for a long time, but it's mostly because Raveena is still on the loose. She still has your voice hidden somewhere, and so far Adriyel and the sorcerers have been unable to recover it. Not to mention the fact that the sorcerers have been on their own ever since Adriyel came to The Academy to train Jael."

I don't understand what it is Raveena hopes to accomplish. Why does she want to be royal sorceress so badly?

Taryn was silent, and his expression made me think he was debating whether or not to tell me. After a while, he finally took a deep breath. "Because, technically, the throne is supposed to be hers."

For a moment, I thought I'd hallucinated. *What?*

"It's a long story. In short, she was the apprentice of Danton, the royal sorcerer before Adriyel, the one who led us in the wars against Windylow. She was top student at The Academy, and was therefore chosen to learn from him."

Are you saying that Raveena was in line to take Danton's place as the king's sorcerer?

Taryn nodded. "Exactly. Just like Jael is now. Apparently, she was an extremely talented sorceress. But as her power grew, Danton began to see that she was not interested in maintaining peace in Arheynia, but simply wanted power. Adriyel soon took her place as apprentice, and Raveena was sent away from the kingdom."

That's why Raveena is always threatening Adriyel and the Royal Army. Not only is she holding a grudge against them, but she still believes the throne is rightfully hers.

"And not only has that put Adriyel, the Army, and the king in danger, but the students at The Academy as well...especially Jael. He's soon to take the position Raveena has been after for years."

I thought a moment.

Taryn's glanced at me questioningly. "Nhanni?"

It was Raveena, wasn't it?

"What do you mean?"

Oh Adriyel...

"Nhanni, what are you talking about?"

It was Raveena. She was the sorceress who killed the girl Adriyel loved, wasn't she?

Taryn was silent, and it was answer enough.

I always wondered how she could possibly be threatened by me when I was only a child. Does it have something to do with the fact that Adriyel and my father are friends?

"Most likely. Raveena probably feared that *you* would become Adriyel's apprentice. She stole your voice to weaken your powers. Of course, this all happened before the prophecy became known. Now Jael is Raveena's target. To be honest…I'm surprised she hasn't tried to harm him yet."

We sat in silence a moment before I realized something else, and turned back to Taryn. *If I'm no longer her target, why hasn't she returned my voice?*

"Raveena is not the type of person who does that, Nhanni. Just because she found out about the prophecy, she wouldn't apologize or give Adriyel what he seeks. She's not that noble. And also…the fact that she has your voice is the only thing keeping the Army from arresting her right this second."

You're a terrible liar, I replied. *You're not telling me everything. I know you aren't.*

He let his shoulders fall. "Your father wanted to keep this from you for as long as possible. But now that you've asked, I'm not going to lie to you."

I nodded, smiling to show my gratitude.

"We don't think Raveena even realised this until after it happened, but when she stole your voice…it didn't just weaken your power. There is a reason Adriyel has been your mentor these past few years, he's been keeping you safe all this time."

I couldn't hide my confusion at this.

"Raveena stole your voice, and your voice is a part of *you*, so naturally it holds magic."

Then I understood. *You mean…when Raveena stole my voice she gained the power that I lost?*

"Yes."

And you and Adriyel think that she might try to steal more of my power?

He hesitated. "Yes."

I buried my face in my hands. *Oh, confound it all!*

*****

I groaned, and fell across the seats as Taryn peered through the open door. "You're going to have to come out of the carriage eventually."

I groaned even louder, and he grinned, grabbing my arm. "Come on."

I rolled over with a glare in his direction, but let him pull me to my feet. He shut the door, paying the coachman, and laughed at my expression as he led me towards The Academy. "Welcome back."

Great...school.

"It won't be *that* bad."

Yes it will. We're going to be sparring for the rest of the year. We all know how well that went the first time.

"You'll get better each time you fight. The last time was just bad luck. You were up against Morahn, and he didn't seem to comprehend that the fight was over once you were down. That, or he didn't care."

I know. I can easily avoid another accident like that one. What worries me is that I can't avoid those certain people who spend time by the lake.

Taryn didn't come up with a reply for this. He led me toward the classroom in silence. "Thought we'd just check in before going to our rooms," he said once we were near, to change the subject.

I noticed then that I hadn't brought my bag, and started to turn back. I left my bag in the carriage

"No problem," Taryn replied. "The carriage is probably still there. Just meet me at Adriyel's office."

I nodded, and ran through the empty halls to the main doors. I approached the carriage again, finding my bag still sitting on the seat. I thanked the coachman as I grabbed it. I was heading back toward the doors when a familiar voice stopped me.

"Nhanni!"

I spun toward the sound reflexively, and realized my mistake too late. The second I saw that it was Jael, I immediately wanted to turn back. But I'd met his gaze, and it was too late now to keep walking and pretend I didn't hear him.

He was ten times more attractive than I remembered, and I found myself blushing as he closed the door to his carriage. He smiled, but seemed a bit hesitant as he came up to me, matching my discomfort.

"I was hoping I would run into you. I know you're probably still mad about our argument at the lake, but I just wanted to apologize and make sure you're doing okay."

I folded my arms across my chest. He was uncomfortably close. When I didn't move, he reached out and touched my arm. "Please talk to me, Nhanni."

I'm fine, I replied as calmly as possible, aware that I was breathing noticeably fast. *I know it wasn't your fault. I just...I just got angry when you lied to Adriyel about your real reasons for wanting to help me.*

To everyone. I can't accept you as a true friend if you can't accept it yourself. You're too caught up in a sense of...of pride, a sense of superiority that you and your friends share.

"I'm sorry," he replied. "But despite what you think I'm not like that anymore. I don't just care about my powers and what people think of me. And after what happened by the lake, I told Gabe and the others to stay away from you."

A lot of good that did the first time! I thought to myself, then pushed my thoughts once more. *I really want to believe you, Jael. But no one can completely change who they are so quickly.*

"I know. I understand if you still don't believe me."

If you truly are different, what happened in so short a time? I asked, less angry now, and more confused. *What changed you?*

"I guess *you* did."

I lost my concentration a moment, my body tensed. *What?* I managed once I pulled myself together.

Jael was silent a moment, glancing away. "It's because I realized that all these ideas, these visions I had of who you were before we met, are so different from who you really are. I made all these assumptions, I never thought we could be friends, and that's why I was so surprised...surprised by how easy it is to like you."

Jael–

"Being your friend seems like the easiest thing in the world now," he continued, his bright smile returning. "I realised that if I hadn't ended up as your partner that day, I may have never even met you. I've always been friends with the athletic students, the popular students, but after I met you I knew I wanted to be better. I knew that instead of spending my time trying to impress people I don't even want to be like, I should spend time with the people I admire."

Admire? I asked him, amazed. *Me?*

"You don't need to impress anyone, *be* anyone, but yourself. You inspire people, show them that what people think of you doesn't matter half as much as what you think of yourself."

He took a step forward. "I wanted to tell you I'm done lying, Nhanni. I'm sorry I ever did, and I hope you'll forgive me. And that…we can still be friends."

He held my gaze a long time, not breaking the silence, and for some reason my eyes watered. *You can't do that, Jael!*

He looked confused. "What?"

After everything that's happened you can't just say you're sorry, and you're done lying! You can't expect to be instantly forgiven!

"I-"

And you can't just come out and say it's easy to like me, and you admire me, and I inspire people! You know you can't feel that way about me!

I started to pull away and he took my hand. "Please just-"

You can't! I interrupted, before he could say anything that might stop me from leaving. I backed away again, turning and preparing to run. *You just can't.*

I heard him take a deep breath. "Nhanni wait!"

He grabbed my arm and pulled me back before I could even think to resist.

Then he kissed me.

I had never kissed a boy before, no more than a small peck on the cheek, and I stood pathetically motionless as his arms tightened around me. When he finally pulled away I stared I remained utterly speechless. He just stared back, his eyes intense but his expression unreadable. We stood, frozen, and when he leaned forward again I quickly stumbled away from him.

He stepped toward me, his hand reaching for mine. "Nhanni-"

I did the only thing I could do.

I ran.

Chapter fourteen

Nhanni

I don't know how long I was sprawled across my bed with my face buried in my pillow. The minutes passed long. My head filled with voices that rang like pounding bells. It felt like forever before I heard the door rattle, then creak open.

I didn't look up; I didn't have to. I knew who it was.

"What happened to meeting me at Adriyel's office?" Taryn asked sarcastically, sitting next to me on the bed.

I sighed, wiping my eyes, before I finally rolled over and took his hand. *I'm sorry. I didn't mean to leave you waiting or to worry you, I just couldn't...I had to be alone for a while.*

"What happened?" he asked. I could tell he was trying his best not to look worried. "Want to talk about it?'

Definitely not.

"It was Gabe, wasn't it?"

I looked away, unable to reply or look him in the eye.

He squeezed my hand tightly. "It's worse than that… it was *Jael*."

I'm fine, Taryn.

"Tell me what he did. Please Nhanni."

I told you, I'm fine, I replied, turning back and meeting his gaze. *He's just...not who I thought he was. I'll most likely be avoiding him for the rest of the year.*

He pulled my hand until I sat up, putting his arm around me. "I'm sorry, Nhanni. I know the two of you were friends. But maybe it's for the best."

I know.

We were silent a long time. Taryn's pale eyes were burning with an intense stare. When I said nothing more, he reached beside the bed and picked up a small package. "Here. Adriyel said it arrived in the mail a bit late; your birthday present from your father."

I smiled as I opened the package. It contained another leather journal, like the one Adriyel had given me. It was absolutely beautiful, and arrived just in time, as my other journal was almost full of words. And now, I had more to say.

I'll have to reply. Tell him thanks.

"You can write to him, but it'll have to wait. We start training again tomorrow, and you should get some sleep. You look exhausted."

I nodded, and pulled the blankets over me without bothering to change out of my clothes.

Taryn stepped into the hallway with a smile. "See you in class tomorrow."

The door closed. I reached up to shut the curtains and darkness instantly filled the room.

The moment I was asleep, the dream came again.

*****

Fears

-To be close
-Letting someone in. We are hurt more easily from near than afar
-To leap off solid ground, and leave behind all I know
-Taking a chance, losing others...or even myself

The darkness around me had been overcome by light, flying over my head like shooting stars.
Soaring just out of reach, tempting me to leap, but I was too afraid I'd fall.

I closed my journal with a sigh and decided I should go to class, even though I hadn't been planning to. Not only would I have to face Jael if I went, but Taryn as well. I didn't know how long I would be able to keep this from him, and Adriyel too.

I hadn't even told them about the lake incident yet, how I had seen it all in a dream before it happened. And now there was the recurring vision of the crowd and the golden staff.

I just didn't know how to tell them I was having more prophetic dreams, and strange and dangerous ones at that. Adriyel made it clear that it wasn't normal, and telling him would only worry him more.

And I couldn't possibly tell them about Jael. It was bad enough that he'd fallen for me.

I couldn't fall for *him* too.

I made it to the ballroom just as the bell rang, and joined the crowd of people that surrounded the teachers. I spotted Taryn in the crowd and went to his side. Taryn smiled as I came up beside him, but there was concern in his eyes.

"Good morning, students," Adriyel said, looking pleased. "We are going to continue sparring. And, as promised, Eldyn and I decided to modify the rules after we saw how much everyone was improving."

"And…" Eldyn added. "We were so impressed by Taryn and Jael's demonstrations of advanced spells that we decided to be very…open-minded. We will allow all of you to use *any* spell from the class spellbook that you can possibly summon."

Adriyel smiled. "We are hoping to see more hidden talent, so give it your very best. Good luck everyone, and let the matches begin!"

The class cheered, excited by the unexpected changes to the rules. This time almost everyone stood on tiptoe, hands raised, hoping to be picked.

In just the first few rounds, I could tell that the rest of the sparring classes would be much more interesting than the first few. Most students could summon some pretty tricky spells; the invisibility spell, attack and defense spells, and some could conjure summoning and sending spells. A boy from Eldyn's class even used a trapping spell, just like Jael had.

"Well done!" Adriyel laughed, glancing around the circle to chose the next two fighters. His eyes rested on me, and he smiled. "Nhanni? Are you willing to try again?"

Someone groaned, most likely one of Jael's friends, and received a glare from Eldyn.

"That's enough!" Adriyel snapped. "Nhanni is just as powerful as any of you, if not *more,* because of the strength it takes her to summon spells. Come on up, Nhanni."

I nodded, and made my way to the center next.

"Come and supervise, Taryn," Adriyel added.

Taryn nodded thankfully, following behind me and clutching my hand tight.

Adriyel scanned the crowd, his eyes resting on someone else. To my horror, I realized it was Jael. "You too, Jael."

I sighed in relief when I understood that Jael was watching, and not *fighting* me.

"Sonya, you will be her opponent."

Sonya showed mixed feelings at being chosen, but nodded without argument.

I came to the center of the open sparring circle and took a deep breath, raising my hands in front of me. Sonya did the same. I nodded to Adriyel that I was ready, though I didn't feel I was.

"Go!" he shouted.

Immediately Sonya sent her best spells at me. "*Incurro!*"

I returned with a quick defense and followed by taking aim with every spell I knew, but she easily avoided anything I threw at her.

We sent our magic swirling back and forth for a while, looking equally matched, before she grinned. "*Creo!*"

I was caught dodging an attack, which I thought was coming toward me. Instead, I ran into the rock she'd created and fell backward. She was starting to use strategy instead of just force.

"*Incurro!*"

I rolled to avoid the next attack and quickly got to my knees, my breath becoming quick gasps, my heart accelerating. I caught a glimpse of her to my left and sent a trapping spell toward her, hoping desperately that my magic was strong enough. Sonya let out a shriek as chains formed around her, and I smiled in triumph as she fell over.

"A *trapping spell*! Wonderful Nhanni!" Adriyel slapped Eldyn on the back in his excitement, and received a glare in response.

The rest of the class, to my surprise, clapped and cheered.

I stood and cautiously stepped towards Sonya, my hands raised in case she attacked. She struggled against the chains at first, but when she saw me approaching she took a deep breath. "*Eximo*!"

I froze. *She knows the spell to counter it.*

Sonya saw I was surprised and took the opportunity to leap to her feet. "*Absconditus*!"

Oh no.

She vanished in an instant, and wisely stayed silent while I spun in circles aimlessly.

"*Incurro*!"

A spiral of orange light flew toward me and I barely had enough time to move out of the way before she attacked again. She kept moving around the circle, making it impossible for me to find her. I was hit with her spell once, but Taryn raised a shield to weaken it and I managed to get back on my feet.

"Adriyel..." I heard Jael say.

"She is doing just fine."

"Please," Taryn asked. "Stop the fight before she gets hurt again."

"Just watch."

Adriyel seemed confident that I would succeed, so I closed my eyes and listened intently, hoping Sonya would make some sort of sound. I smiled to myself as I raised my hands and created more rocks all around the circle. It was my turn to strategize.

I heard a loud 'thump!'. It was Sonya tripping over one of the rocks, and I spun towards the sound. I sent a visibility spell forward and she appeared before me, her knotted eyebrows and gaping mouth showing how displeased she was that I had found her.

"*Exitium!*"

All of the rocks vanished and we circled each other, throwing attack spells again. My power was quickly draining, and knew I had to end the fight soon or I wouldn't have any strength left. One of Sonya's attack spells hit me like the force of a wall and the shock of electricity at the same time. Even dulled by the shields raised before me, the spell took its toll. I fell to my knees. Already, I was panting to catch my breath.

Then a word popped into my head, one that I had probably read in the class spellbook. I knew what spell it was, and that there was a very good chance it would fail, but I also knew that I only had a second before Sonya attacked again.

I raised my hands, summoning the very last of my power.

Accendo!

I expected blue magic that sped toward her, but it was something else entirely. The entire room, including the teachers, gasped.

Fire.

Somehow I had used an elemental spell against her; a spell that very few magicians could ever learn, let alone succeed in summoning. And somehow... I had done it without even trying.

"*Contego!*"

Adriyel's deep red magic blocked my attack at the last moment, shielding Sonya from the blue-tinted flames. She was forced backward even though the spell had been stopped. I sat back, gasping, as Adriyel, Edlyn, Taryn, and Jael ran toward me.

"Nhanni," Adriyel said, slowly kneeling next to me. "How on *earth-?*"

I don't know.

Adriyel's face turned even whiter. "Did you...did you just use a *Mens Mentis* without physical contact?"

"What?" Taryn said, managing to look amazed and outraged at the same time. "Adriyel that's impossible! She's only an *apprentice!*"

"Even more impossible than prophetic dreams?" Jael asked them. "Even more impossible than the *fire* we just saw her summon?"

"It *is* in the spellbook, but I never thought a mere student could summon an *element*," Eldyn added.

Jael nodded. "Even I can't."

They all stared at me. I couldn't help but shy away from all of their gazes, suddenly very self-conscious.

"Class dismissed!" Adriyel called, and students began filing out the doors with soft murmurs, which sounded of confusion.

I remained silent as Adriyel stared at me again, his eyes serious. "I think you and I should talk, Nhanni."

But I don't know anything, I protested.

Adriyel helped me to my feet, and Jael stepped forward when he saw me almost lose balance. "Adriyel, don't you think you should at least let Nhanni rest first?"

Taryn glared in his direction, his arm steadying me.

Adriyel sighed. "Yes, you are right. You should have known that summoning such advanced spells, especially without words of power, would really wear you out, Nhanni."

The room started spinning.

"You used a great deal of magic," Adriyel continued. "In fact, I am surprised you have not-"

"Nhanni!" Taryn gasped.

My legs failed and I fell, conscious only of Taryn's arms catching me before I hit the floor.

Chapter fifteen

When I regained consciousness, for only a moment, I could feel familiar arms around me. I could tell that he was running as he carried me down the hall.

Taryn?

"You're okay, Nhanni. You just need to rest."

The bright lights flashing across my closed eyelids began to fade, and the arms carrying me vanished as if turning into mist. There was a cold, stone surface under me now, and I began to feel small patters of rain on my exposed skin.

I heard footsteps coming down the stone path. I didn't open my eyes as they stopped right beside me, and familiar arms scooped me up.

"Nhanni…" his velvet voice whispered. "I'm so sorry."

Taryn-

"Shhh…just sleep."

I let sleep find me again, the lights behind my eyes dimming and becoming frozen images that flashed in blurs too quickly for me to keep up.

There were several large mirrors pushed up against the walls, and the room was lit by the hugest fireplace I'd ever seen, flickering with deep-purple flames. There was something ominous about the place; I could hear a soft crying sound like small whispering voices from beneath the floor and behind the walls.

I was beginning to lose track of what was dream, and what was reality. I could still feel Taryn's arms around me, and I could still feel the small droplets of rain clinging to my skin and soaking through my clothes. I could hear the soft crackling of a fire, and the voices whispering from the far corners of the room.

Jael turned away from me slowly, and approached the fireplace with heavy steps like he was sleepwalking. Raveena grinned as Jael raised his hands toward the flames, the medallion around his neck glowing with vibrant light. The flames flickered wildly, growing and glowing more brightly. The soft whispers grew louder, reaching a crescendo until they reverberated in my ears like bells.

I felt a small tug as I was pulled into the mirror, melting through the surface and coming into darkness. I searched aimlessly for a light in the room, and fire suddenly jumped and bounced from the dark corners as if chasing me away.

Tiny figures leapt from the flames, human-like but made of fire. They danced around the room like walking suns.

I stepped through the mirror once again, relieved to discover I was once again behind the walls of The Academy, safely resting in the protection of Taryn's arms.

Adriyel gasped as I grabbed Jael's hand, placing the ring in his palm. "It is destiny. I was meant to give it to you all along."

It wasn't till I was pulled from the last vision that I realized I was walking. Even though I'd been sleeping I'd ended up in the doorway to Adriyel's office, still in bare feet and wearing my thin nightdress. I could hear soft whispers once again, and I shivered as my feet kept walking as if they had a mind of their own. I was approaching his desk, my hand reaching out to the small crystal ball resting on the corner. Images blurred behind the glass surface, flashing in and out of focus too quickly for me to catch much detail, just as it had been while I was dreaming.

"The sorcerer to wield *Dust of the stars*
And all the power it may bring
Shall earn a place on a palace thrown
As sorcerer of Arheynia's king"

The prophecy...I knew it well, but what did the crystal mean by reciting it to me now? Why had it called me here?

The voices grew louder as I watched the images change, and I could make out only a tall figure in a small, cluttered room. I immediately recognized him as the Oracle, clad in the familiar cloak pulled over his head and casting his face in shadows.

He was reaching toward his own crystal ball as it swirled with coloured smoke and flashed with light. As I watched, a small smile pulled at the corner of his mouth. "It is time."

The moment I opened my eyes, I reached for my journal and pen, sending piles of papers flying off of my desk. I squinted in the dim light streaming through the window, and took a deep breath before I began writing.

The smoky air was like a screen twisting my vision, warm foggy fingers clawing at my eyes and lungs. The heat was intense and uncomfortable, boring down like boiling water being poured from the sky. My breath escaped in quick gasps as my throat swallowed the air despite its dry, cracked walls.

I searched aimlessly for a palm tree, or a pool of clear water, anything besides the waves of rock and sand shaping the earth's ocean, anything besides the thick brown haze my eyes squinted through. I wandered desperately, but there was nothing to be found. When you are lost, you are lost.

There was no map, no water, no shade, no hope...only the harsh rays of sun pushing down on me, its weight only growing heavier before I collapsed under it.

In the depth of my despair a voice reached me, the imagined call of a soft silk wind lightly brushing my consciousness, its voice steadily increasing until it was a roar in my ears. Eclipsed eyes opened, squinting in sharp rays of sunlight that pierced like painful blades at my eyes. Slowly I made out a shape.

A face.

A smile; and a hand helping me to my far-traveled feet. An angel unexpectedly and inexplicably appearing from the ocean's depths, rising over the waves and pulling me from the tide's icy grasp.

An angel's smile shining light onto a mind cast into shadows, so far lost only to return with the gentle nudge of a voice. An angel I leaned against as I limped through the desert's tides, catching a glimpse of wonderous green and blue amongst the hazy golden dunes. A hope suddenly renewed, a determination suddenly lifted from the ashes of his words.

I follow him.

An illusion, or a paradise brought to light through the thick, smoky haze of despair.

I follow.

A tide washing me to the safe haven of shore, or pulling me deeper into the black void of the ocean.

I follow.

An angel, or the sweet invention of a hopeless dream.

I follow.

I read over the squiggly letters, my eyes catching words that I hadn't even realised I'd written. Then, remembering the confusing flashes of dreams that now kept me awake, I turned the page over and picked up my pen again.

A dream within a dream is dangerous when you wake up. In the real world now, you sometimes don't know what to believe. Because it feels exactly the same, almost as if real life is just another dream. Just another world invented and created by our imaginings.

The only way to tell the dream is over...is time. In dreams time moves quickly, sped up in second-long glimpses like hundreds of tableaus flashing to life. Time is broken and confusing in dreams, skipping ahead and back again.
That is how one can tell reality; when time moves forward at a constant pace. When there is no more chaos and for a moment our lives are steady.

The problem with dreams within a dream is that when you wake up...the dream itself becomes more steady than before. Perhaps not quite as steady as reality, but steady enough to trick the mind into thinking it's awake. Before long, after waking from more than one dream, it makes one begin to wonder: Are we ever truly awake?

Or is life just another dream...just one over which we have more control.

Chapter sixteen

Jael

I didn't move my eyes off of the landscape, even after I heard a second bell ring. I was sitting on one of the stone benches lining the narrow corridors, staring out of the giant second-story window. I wasn't keeping track of time, but I was sure everyone would be leaving the lake by now.

I'd been sitting here ever since class ended, and now the sun was beginning to set behind rows of red and pink coloured clouds. I was beginning to regret what I'd done, now that I'd remembered why Adriyel always told me to focus on my studies instead of girls. The only reason I'd been safe from sorcerers who would see me as a threat was because, till now, they'd had no way of hurting me. Or threatening me.

I should have thought about what I was doing.

I should have recognised that the people in life that I try to hold onto the most, will be the ones that I'm more likely to lose. I was beginning to see Nhanni as the person I wanted to be with, the person who made me better, but all of the enemies I hadn't met yet…they would see Nhanni as nothing but a weakness.

I sighed, my thoughts so loud in my head that I didn't hear anyone approaching until Gabe stood right beside me. He shoved my feet aside and sat down on the bench with a glare. "That's the third time in a row you've skipped dinner, Jael."

I rolled my head away, looking back out the window. "I'm guessing they're mad."

"Not really," Gabe replied, resting his head against the wall. "We're worried about you, all of us. Even Adriyel. Since the long weekend you do nothing but sigh and stare out of windows. What is up with you?"

I faced forward. "I'm just stressed. In a few months I'm supposed to be the king's sorcerer…and I'm not sure I want that kind of responsibility."

"Who are you trying to fool? Everyone knows that you've been waiting for this your entire life, Jael."

When I didn't say anything, he took a deep breath and met my gaze. "And we also know the *real* reason you've been acting like this."

"Why would you ask if you already know?"

"I want to hear you say it."

My shoulders fell. The hallway was dead silent, not even the sound of distant footsteps, and I assumed now that classes were over everyone would be in their rooms or having dinner.

And no one would hear us.

"I lied," I finally admitted, my voice lowering automatically even though he was the only one there. "Nhanni…is not just my partner." His face, to my disappointment, was hard as stone. He didn't show any sign of emotion; not surprise, anger, relief, or even disapproval. When he still didn't speak after some time, I let out another exasperated sigh. "I'm in *so* much trouble…"

"How could you be so stupid, Jael? And *Nhanni*, of all people."

"You don't know her, Gabe. She's nothing like what everyone thinks," I replied. "I tried to stay away from her, to ignore my feelings, but I couldn't."

He rolled his eyes, staring out the window. I followed his gaze, watching as the sky slowly darkened, my eyes resting on the horizon, hoping I would find all the answers there. I didn't know why I told Gabe the truth in that moment, or why I thought he'd be any help.

When the silence had dragged on for too long, I sighed to myself. "Why am I even telling *you* this?"

"You do know what this means, right? If anyone finds out, she'll be in danger. You aren't on the throne yet, but you still have more enemies than you think."

"I know."

"We can't let anyone find out," Gabe said, and turned back to me as if searching for some sort of understanding or approval in my gaze.

I stared at the floor, aware of the heat rising to my cheeks. "Umm...Nhanni kind of knows."

"What?" he gasped, his eyes expanding. "You *told* her?"

"Not exactly..."

"This is *not* happening. You did *not-*"

"Yeah. I kind of... *kissed* her."

Gabe's fist connected with my arm. "You *idiot!*"

"*Owww.*"

"You can't just *kiss* her, you don't want to confuse her *more!*"

"It's a bit late for that. She's been avoiding me since."

Gabe sat back with another huge sigh, his face finally showing some emotion. "*Unbelievable...*"

We sat in silence a long time, our breaths slowing as a calm gradually fell over us.

"What are you going to do?" he finally asked.

I glanced at him in confusion, unable to hide my obvious surprise that he would even ask this question. He was showing a different side of himself; a side I'd never seen before. "It doesn't matter if Nhanni feels the same or not. There's no way we can be together."

He met my gaze.

"Why do you care all of a sudden, Gabe?" I asked.

"Because I made a mistake a while ago, the very same mistake you're about to make."

"What are you talking about?"

"I fell for a girl," he said, his usually hard eyes filling with moisture. "A girl I couldn't have. But instead of fighting for her, I let her go."

I was frozen now, staring at him in shock again. "You fell for a girl? *You*?"

"Yeah, yeah, don't sound so surprised."

"Did I know her?"

"No," he replied, taking a deep breath. It looked like he was about to explode; like the sudden amount of secrecy and emotion inside him was too much for him to keep to himself anymore. "She's mortal."

"What?" I asked. I had to make sure I'd heard right. "*What*?"

Gabe sighed. "She's a mortal."

I felt like my eyes were about to pop out of my head. "You had feelings for a *mortal* and you were just calling *me* an idiot?"

"Yeah."

"Do you even understand how against the rules that is? Falling for a *mortal* is on the very top of a sorcerer's *not*-to-do list."

"I know Jael, okay? My parents were furious when I told them. They explained everything, how sorcerers are scarce and none of us can have relationships with mortals, because we cannot risk the disappearance of magic forever. There's just too few of us left."

After a moment, I was calm again, nodding my head sadly when I understood. "Everyone said you can't be together, and you listened."

"Exactly," he replied, blinking mist from his eyes. "I don't want you to live with that regret, like I have. I promise you that if you truly have feelings for Nhanni, you can't ever let her go."

I just stared at him. "You do realize how strange those words sound coming from *you*?"

He chuckled softly, shifting uncomfortably on the stone bench. "You can't blame all of us from trying to stop you from falling for her, but now that it's happened I'm telling you that you can't ignore how you feel."

I stared at the floor. Every time I thought about telling Nhanni, I remembered the story Adriyel told me. I remembered how he'd loved someone, and how she'd been killed over nothing but a small rivalry. "I just…don't want to lose her."

"How do you know you will?" Gabe countered. "I know it might sound horrible, but which way would you rather lose her? By letting her go, or fighting to keep her? Adriyel may regret what happened when he fought that sorceress, but I know for a fact he doesn't have to live with the regret of never telling that girl how he felt."

I nodded to myself and, for the first time in weeks, I smiled. "Thank you, Gabe."

His eyes abruptly turned hard again when he realized that he was being nice. "Not saying it won't be hard, cause it will. If Adriyel finds out that you like her-"

"Yeah," I mumbled, shaking my head. "But I have to tell Nhanni. She's probably so confused. I just...don't know how to say it though."

Gabe cocked his eyebrow. "Something like 'Hi Nhanni, just thought you should know... I really like you'."

"You don't get it. I don't just *like* her, Gabe." I glanced at him finally, stuttering on the words. "I...I think I-"

He took a deep breath, resting his hand on my shoulder with a serious expression. "Oh boy..."

Chapter seventeen

Nhanni

I only left my room for five minutes, assuming I wouldn't run into anyone in the time I was gone. I was returning from the kitchen with my dinner when, as luck would have it, I saw Jael approaching from down the hall.

We both stopped just outside my door, neither of us saying anything; neither of us meeting the other's gaze. Since my *Mens Mentis Pulsus* seemed to work almost on its own now, I knew I had to concentrate on keeping my mind clear.

"Hi," Jael finally said, after a long silence.

I moved towards my door without a word.

"You can't avoid me forever, Nhanni."

I gave up and, instead of retreating into my room, I dropped the plate of food on my dresser and shut the door. I folded my arms as I turned and reluctantly met his gaze.

"And now that you can push your thoughts whenever you want, you no longer have an excuse not to talk to me."

Fine, I replied, sighing in defeat. I'm sorry that I've been avoiding you. It's just...you-

"I know," he said and looked away from me. "I know that you weren't expecting that. I didn't mean to surprise you. I'm sorry."

I nodded. It's fine. It was just a mistake.

"That's not what I meant…" he said with a sad smile. "I'm sorry that you have to feel this way. But, I'm not sorry I kissed you."

I just stared. Another awkward silence passed, and even my thoughts were completely blank.

Jael stared back, slowly stepping forward when he decided I wouldn't say anything. "I know that I'm Adriyel's apprentice and I'm not supposed to love-"

Jael-

"But I can't think of another word to describe how I feel about you."

"Please don't," I said quickly. I looked away, moving toward my door in case I needed to escape.

Jael knew me too well, and stepped forward again. He was right in front of me now, his glassy green eyes wide and intense, and I couldn't meet his gaze. "What are you afraid of, Nhanni?"

You know, Jael. There's a good reason you aren't supposed to have feelings for anyone. If anyone finds out…if Adriyel finds out-

"I thought of that, Nhanni, and at first I did try to put my feelings aside. But a friend of mine made me realize that the only thing I should fear is being apart from you."

You don't get it, Jael, I said, finally glancing up at him. *This whole time Adriyel's been expecting this from you and trying to stop it. Don't you remember what happened when he fell in love?*

Jael's eyes fell, a look of understanding crossing his face. "The girl...the girl who was killed..."

If he has any reason to believe you care about me, you can be sure we'll be kept as far apart as possible.

"I know he's been trying to prevent this, but he can't do anything now. It's too late for that," he replied. "My feelings won't just go away. I will feel the same whether we're together or apart."

*This can't be happening...*I said in my thoughts over and over, more to myself than to Jael. *It's as Adriyel said...Raveena has been waiting for the perfect opportunity to hurt you. Now she has it.*

His eyes widened when I mentioned her name, and it dawned on me that I'd never considered that he knew who she was.

Does anyone else know? Anyone besides your friend?

"No."

Good, I replied with a relieved sigh. *Then at least we can try and keep it secret.*

"Is that what you really want?" he asked after a moment, looking me in the eye again. "You really think being apart will help?"

What...what do you mean? I stammered, shying away from the piercing gaze.

"I mean, more than just Raveena will be after you. This is *your* battle as much as it is mine now, and we are strongest together."

We can't possibly be *together*, Jael, that's crazy! Besides, how do you even know I feel the same way?

Almost before I even finished speaking, he took my head in his hands and kissed me again. I didn't pull away, I didn't try to stop him, and it wasn't long before I realized I was kissing him back.

After a moment, he released me, and there was a long silence as we stared, unashamed, into each other's eyes.

"That's how I know," he whispered.

I couldn't bring myself to deny it, because I knew that he was right. I did feel the same, I had for a while, but I'd just been too afraid to admit it.

I wasn't anymore.

Jael must have sensed what I was thinking. He smiled slightly and I sighed in defeat as he rested his head against mine.

No one can know, I finally said.

"I know."

What will we do?

"I think it's best we postpone telling Adriyel as long as possible." I managed a smile.

"And…" he continued, pulling away and meeting my gaze. "It doesn't matter what else happens. We'll face it together."

I nodded in agreement, taking a deep breath.

Jael's expression turned thoughtful, his eyes staring off into nothing before they widened.

What?

"Your dream...your dream about the blooming rose."

I froze in shock as I remembered. That's right, it was my first prophetic dream. Adriyel predicted that I would fall in love.

Jael nodded, looking slightly overwhelmed, his mouth unsure whether to smile or to pop open in surprise. "Your prophecy has come true."

Chapter eighteen

Adriyel

The wind howled outside my window, threatening to throw the shutters open and extinguish my last remaining candle stub. The light it gave off was dim, but it was enough to illuminate the worn pages of the spellbooks I was flipping through. My eyes tried to close in exhaustion as they looked over the faint letters, and I knew that I'd read late into the night more than one too many times. I'd been unable to find a spell that could help me and the sorcerers recover Nhanni's voice, one that Raveena had not yet encountered.

A presence hit me then.

It was hard to notice at first, the soft violet aura coming from the glass ball on my desk, and the subtle scent of fresh flowers drifting about the room. I quickly shut my books, and stared at the images slowly taking shape behind the clear, crystal surface. I caught my breath when I saw a glimpse of dark hair and a glassy green eye framed with thick lashes.

"I was not expecting to hear from you...*ever*."

"I'm no fool, Adriyel. I know you've been trying to use my crystal as a looking glass. I've called you to make sure that your little experiments to catch glimpses into my home come to an end."

"Why?" I asked with a small grin, trying to keep my tone as level as possible. "Afraid that I will find where you have hidden Nhanni's voice?"

"The voice of a child? I care nothing for it."

The scent of wild roses hit me, making my head spin. "Really? Because last time I checked…it has been the only thing keeping me and the other sorcerers from crashing through your door for the last seventeen years."

I could see her entirely now, and a glowing smile slowly spread across her face when she caught my expression.
"Are you certain the girl's voice is all you're after? Surely it is something much more important than that?"

"Do not go there, Raveena."

"I hate to reopen old wounds….but I'm beginning to think the little accident with that young girl is still getting to you. You'd like to think you're doing this to save your poor student, but your heart is too full of hatred for me, and the desire for revenge."

"*Accident*?" I couldn't stop my voice from rising to a roar now, and my face from flushing in anger. "I think the word you are looking for is *murder!*"

The hairs on my arms stood on end as she laughed, her voice ringing through the dead of night like a Siren's cry. The small candle on my desk flickered as a small breeze seeped through the clattering shutters.

"You had every opportunity to save her. I gave you the choice; to resign the position I rightfully deserved, or to watch the curse I'd placed on her slowly take hold. You refused to give me what I wanted, and while you took your time seeking the Oracle for his help…the girl suffered. Make no mistake, I never intended for the curse to kill her. I knew her soul was not weak, but I miscalculated the damage her body would have to take."

"All I needed was time…you could have lifted the curse while I tried to find the Oracle! You could have paid for your mistakes once you knew what you had done! But you had to run. And you did notstop there…but did everything in your power to destroy any happiness I had found in my life afterwards. Not only have I suffered for it, but so have Nhanni, and Jael…and everyone else you have taken advantage of!"

A small spark of rage flashed in her eyes. And as she spoke, it sounded as though it was difficult for her to keep her voice calm. "Don't make me the villain, dear Adriyel. Don't forget that you've been keeping secrets from your precious students; the truth about what happened the night your true love died."

Warm tears stung my eyes, and I could feel my heart thudding against the confines of my chest. "It is because of *you* she is dead in the first place! And you know very well that *you* are also the reason I cannot tell him!"

"The boy will never know how you so carefully kept your past hidden in the shadows. And the girl as well…the poor thing shall never have her voice back. And all because of a small mistake you and your sorcerers made long ago. You would've been wise to hand over *Dust of the stars* when I demanded it the first time. Now her voice is safely locked away, and for no reason at all. Such a waste…"

"It was not a waste."

She glanced at me, looking shocked. Determination overtook me, carefully saving the anger building up for the time when I would need it most. "She is getting stronger every day. Her inability to use words makes her very special, makes her able to summon the most difficult spells without even having to rely on words of power. And when her voice is returned, she will be twice as strong as before."

Raveena's face hardened, and I couldn't help but grin in triumph. "And all because of a *small mistake made long ago*. I guess I have *you* to thank for that, Raveena."

Outside, the howling wind died and a strange tranquility fell over The Academy; the storm subsiding just as quickly as it had appeared. As I watched, the aura slowly faded from the crystal, and the sweet scent of flowers became the scent of a burning flame. "Do no call on me again, unless you plan on admitting defeat."

"Don't count on it."

"Excellent," I replied, grinning as her image slowly began to fade. "I will have the pleasure of taking you down myself, then."

Chapter nineteen

Nhanni

A heart can accelerate so quickly.

It can pound against the confines of my chest, yearning to break free with its beats. A heart wants what it wants. I don't get a say in who it chooses to love, who it chooses to trust, and what it chooses to dream. When my mind is screaming in protest, when I try to convince myself otherwise, my heart only becomes more and more persistent.

Like the rain.

No matter how many empty buckets are placed under a leaking roof, they are constantly filling, overflowing, and filling again. The heart can never be empty for long. It is always filling, if only one tiny drop at a time. Seconds become hours, hours become days, and still the rain persists, pattering down on the walls of my confinement, trying to flood me and overtake me with its strength.

But no matter how much I secretly yearn to give into the tide, I fight it with, and against, my own will. Contradicting myself, lying to myself, fighting myself.

It is a battle that cannot be won. A battle I fight knowing all along that I will eventually give in, and surrender. That I will release myself and trust myself with he who has won, placing my love with someone who only makes my uncertainty and vulnerability stronger. With the one person with the power to hurt me, or save me.

I gave in.

I followed the consistent, persistent beating of my heart, like drums forced into a symphony. I followed the thin line between love and devastation, balancing only with the frail instinct of a mind that betrayed me. There is nothing below me but empty space, nothing to catch me but the invented arms of a defeater I know not if I can trust, or if I can love.

There is only the hope that he will catch me when I start to fall, down into the unwelcoming depths of my despair.

"Despair?" Taryn said curiously, looking over my shoulder. "That's dramatic."

I jumped in my chair, unaware that he'd been standing behind me, and quickly slammed my journal shut. Taryn laughed as I spun around with an angry glare.

"Sorry, I couldn't help it."

Mind your own business, Taryn.

"Ok, ok. What's so secret that you can't even tell *me*?"

I slid my journal back into my bag, my cheeks reddening.

Taryn grinned again and cocked his eyebrow at my expression. "You're not secretly crushing on me, are you Nhanni?"

You wish.

"What's in there, then?" he asked, attempting to reach behind me.

Nothing, Taryn.

"Is it more dreams? Come on, let me see!"

No!

I managed to grab both his arms and hold him off, but he was strong and continued to escape my grasp. He laughed and, realizing I wouldn't win, I quickly spun around, snatched my journal from my bag, and turned to face Taryn again.

He only grinned as I held the journal behind my back. No way, Taryn. I write about more than just *dreams* in my journal. It's private.

He reached around me again. "You do realize that only makes me want to read it *more*, right?"

Stop it! I complained.

"Come on, give it!"

No!

I glanced around the classroom nervously, but no one seemed to be paying us any attention. Everyone continued eating their lunches, not bothering to ask what was happening, except for Jael. He was watching us, I now noticed, his expression suggesting he was upset by this display.

Taryn laughed as I backed into a desk, his arms circling me so that I was trapped. "You're *really* protective of that thing. Must be something very embarrassing in there."

Stop! This isn't funny, Taryn!

He almost took hold of the journal, and I gripped it even tighter. As he fought to pull it from my grasp. Taryn's grin spread and I guessed, too late, that someone had come up behind me. The journal was snatched from my hands, and I spun around and frantically tried to grab it back. I saw that Adriyel was the one who took it, and he exchanged a grin with Taryn before opening it about halfway through.

Adriyel, don't-

He was already flipping through my journal, and I caught a breath as I stood silent. He did not read it; he was too kind to do such a thing, unlike Taryn. He simply closed it after he saw for certain that I'd written some new entries.

"Aha! So you *have* been dreaming, Nhanni. You should have told me; I could have tried to decipher more of them."

I took the journal from his hands. *I just forgot. I can show you later.*

Adriyel stared at me with a confused expression. "Grabby. Must be something you do not want me to see."

My face flushed.

"Do not tell me...has your dream come true? Was I right about loverboy?" Adriyel asked with a wink.

I didn't reply, and he burst into roaring laughter. "It has happened all right! It is written all over your face!"

No! It wasn't him! It's nothing!

"I see. You must have let him down, the poor boy."

"Who?" Taryn asked, his eyes wide.

Adriyel shrugged. "I do not know. She would not tell me."

Taryn faced me. "Who? Who was it, Nhanni? Did someone...you know-?"

I said it was nothing!

Taryn stood frozen, his face turning pale. "Wait a second..."

Adriyel stepped towards him, and he seemed alarmed by Taryn's expression. "What Taryn?" he asked.

"That day after the long weekend-"

Taryn-

He looked horrified now. "*Jael?*"

"*What?*" Adriyel roared.

Taryn please-

He ignored me, pushing past Adriyel and stalking across the classroom towards Jael.

"Taryn! Not here!" Adriyel called. When we realized he wouldn't stop, we quickly followed after him, forcing our way through groups of oblivious students.

"You *idiot*!" Taryn roared, shoving Jael roughly while the rest of the class watched with stunned expressions. "How could you do this to her?"

Jael raised his hands defensively. "Please let me explain, Taryn-"

"Adriyel made it very clear that you were to keep your distance! *I* made it very clear! You have *no idea* what you've done!"

"I know this wasn't supposed to happen, and I never wanted to get her involved! I didn't even mean to kiss her the first time, it just-"

Jael's eyes widened when he understood what he'd just said, and his words were cut off when Taryn's fist connected with his jaw.

"Taryn!" Adriyel called again, trying to pull him back.

I tried to grab his arm, stepping between him and Jael. Taryn only shoved me and Adriyel away, and came at Jael again. Jael dodged and tackled Taryn to the floor, where they continued to throw fists at each other. I could only watch in horror, like the rest of the class, while Adriyel tried his best to pull them apart.

Finally, I couldn't take it anymore. "STOP!" I shrieked in my head.

The entire class of students screamed and covered their ears, their wide eyes turning to me. Jael glanced up at me, his expression softening, before Adriyel pulled him to his feet. Jael yanked his arm away, glaring at Taryn as he stood.

Taryn still looked furious. "You'll pay for this-!"

Adriyel shoved Taryn back. "That is enough!"

"She's in danger because of you!"

"I said *enough*!" Adriyel grabbed Taryn's arm and shoved him towards his desk.

After a moment, he sighed and turned back. "Taryn, Jael, I would like to speak with you."

Jael moved towards his desk, and Adriyel's gaze rested on me. "And you, Nhanni."

I nodded, my face falling and my cheeks reddening in embarrassment. The class stared.

"The rest of you are free to go! There will be no afternoon class today!"

The students began to leave, whispering intently amongst themselves as they shuffled out the doors.

"Did Jael and Taryn just get into a fist fight...over *Nhanni*?" I heard Sonya ask Amberly as I passed.

I lowered by eyes and continued forward without meeting their gaze.

Amberly's eyes widened. "I think they *did*."

"I don't know," Jael explained, for the hundredth time, his eyes lowered. "It just happened."

Adriyel was back in his anxiety routine. He was still pacing back and forth in front of his desk, shaking his head wildly. "I do not *believe* this…"

"What will we do?" Taryn asked him. Though he was slightly more calm, his face was still hard. "The entire class knows; probably the entire *Academy* by now. And pretty soon, Jael's enemies will find out too."

"I know," Adriyel muttered.

"This is exactly why we were trying to *avoid* this, *Jael*."

"There's nothing either of you can do," Jael said, his eyes resting on me. "I love her."

"*Do not* say that," Adriyel roared.

"It's the truth. You can't change it."

I shook my head at Jael, and he silenced when he saw that he was only making it worse. There was a long silence, Adriyel's eyes moving constantly, exchanging glances with Jael and I.

Taryn looked furious, but spoke quietly. "Adriyel?"

When I met his gaze, Adriyel looked surprisingly calm. He sighed in defeat after a moment, and glanced at Taryn seriously. "Enough, Taryn. Jael has admitted that he made a mistake. It will do no good to torture him for it now."

"But-!"

"We cannot stay angry about something that happened in the past. Our only concern now is how to keep Nhanni safe."

Taryn relaxed and finally nodded.

I sat back in my chair. As much as it was bothering me that they were talking about me, as if I wasn't there, I didn't want to contribute to this particular conversation.

"Are we sure anyone would risk attacking her while she's here, Adriyel?" Jael asked him. "You are royal sorcerer, after all. Who out there would ever challenge *you*?"

Taryn and Adriyel both shook their heads.

"There are many, surprisingly enough. I will send for your father immediately, Nhanni. I think it best we move you to the palace as soon as possible. There is no safer place in all Arheynia."

I nodded, and went back to staring at the floor.

"And me as well, Adriyel."

"Taryn-"

"You said yourself that my magic surpasses even *yours*! If you must accompany Nhanni to the palace in order to protect her, then I will as well."

"Taryn, because Jael has not finished his apprenticeship with me yet, he too will have to come to the palace," Adriyel explained. "Can you promise me there'll be no more fighting between you two if I bring you *both* along?"

Taryn and Jael exchanged a glance, their eyes narrow.

Please guys...I sighed, hoping they could both hear me.

"Don't look at *me*, Taryn's the one who attacked first," Jael muttered.

"You could have ended the fight anytime, Jael, but you were only too eager to hit him back."

"*Fine*," Jael agreed, his eyes rolling slightly before he glanced at me.

Taryn nodded reluctantly.

"Alright, then," said Adriyel. He finally relaxed and stopped his pacing, falling in his chair with a sigh "We will leave as soon as Rowyn arrives. All three of you need to be ready."

We nodded.

There was a long silence, except for the flames flickering in the fireplace. Jael fidgeted with the huge medallion around his neck, and Adriyel flipped through the pages of my journal, which was resting on his desk. A steady breeze rattled the tall windows, and somewhere in the distance a raven cawed.

At last Adriyel glanced at me and broke the silence.

"I noticed that you managed to push your thoughts towards the entire class earlier," he noted, releasing an impressed puff of air. "Your powers are getting stronger every day."

"It still doesn't make sense…how your *Mens Mentis* is so strong, how you had a prophetic dream, and how you summoned an element," Taryn said quietly.

Adriyel had turned back to my journal, absentmindedly flipping through the pages again. He stopped suddenly with a gasp, and we all turned to face him, confused by his reaction.

"Nhanni!" Adriyel said in surprise, motioning towards the journal. "You had a dream of drowning?"

I stopped still. *Oh yeah…I guess I forgot to tell you about that.*

"Drowning? You mean you had a dream like that *before* the lake incident?" Taryn said in surprise.

I shied away from his gaze. Jael gasped. "Impossible…*another* prophetic dream."

Adriyel came around his desk. "How many dreams like this have you had, Nhanni?"

I can't remember all of my dreams, I replied as he stood beside me. *But I do remember one…where I am standing before a crowd and holding a staff.*

Adriyel started pacing again, looking deep in thought. "Incredible, just incredible. Your dreams are no longer abstract, like the rose; this is the real thing."

"Can you decipher it, Adriyel?" Taryn asked.

"No, not this dream. It could possibly be normal, and not prophetic at all. Perhaps it does see into the future, but that would mean the meaning is quite literal. Did you see anyone you know in the dream, Nhanni?"

My cheeks reddened. Only Jael.

Everyone stared at me in surprise. Jael sat up in his chair, his eyes meeting mine, full of wonder.

He was one of the people in the crowd, I explained when no one said anything.

"Well?" Taryn finally asked.

Adriyel looked stunned. "It appears Nhanni's dreams do indeed allow her to glimpse the future."

Jael shook his head. "But that means-"

"I know," Adriyel said, his gaze resting on me.

Everything was silent; the wind and raven could once again be heard from outside. A lifetime seemed to pass before Adriyel finally spoke.

"Nhanni...you are *not* a sorceress," he said, his voice sombre and almost regretful. "You are an Oracle."

Book three

Chapter twenty

Nhanni

Time rarely moves at the pace we want it to. It is always moving too fast, or too slow. Or is it us who move too quickly; too slowly? Are we wasting precious time trying to fill the hours of the day with something, and then trying to save hours of the day whenever there don't seem to be enough?

If we should treasure anything in life, it should be our time. Whether it's moments we spend in stillness, or moments when we're constantly in motion. The state of our mind affects the way we perceive it. If I tell myself that today I will finish something I've started, or today I will take a risk, I am more likely to really do so than if I start the day off with regret.

We need to know what we have before it's gone, and know what we can have if we make the most of things. We need to know there is a plan for us, a destiny, but a destiny that will not shape itself. We need to know that what is important is not the time in our lives, but the life we live in our time.

Those without fear can take steps that aren't slowed by hesitance; can take in the song and choreograph the dance almost in the same instant. When we are certain of our destination, we do not need to see our path. We can traverse without maps, wander without a fixed path, and see without eyes.

We find ourselves when there are no footsteps to follow, when there is only ambition, a built-in sense of direction, to guide us.

I glanced nervously at Adriyel. He stared, unblinking, at the crystal sphere on his desk, his lips pulled together and his gaze intense. It was as if he was no longer in the same room, as if he'd literally been pulled into the images flashing before him and left his empty body sitting upright in the chair.

I sighed again, impatient to hear what it was Adriyel was seeing. Taryn flashed me a warning glance. "We can't interrupt him while he's watching. It's the same as the looking glass that your father gave us; he is here *literally,* but his mind is wandering the visions that the crystal is showing him. If we pull him out before he's done, he may forget everything he's seen."

I'm just worried. He's been staring at that crystal for a long time.

We all turned when Adriyel caught a breath, his eyes closing. He sighed heavily before glancing tiredly in our direction. "It is the same as before, I am afraid. I cannot see any more of my surroundings, and I am not even close to finding your voice Nhanni. Raveena has hidden it well."

"She certainly has. I didn't see anything either," Jael added.

None of us spoke for a while, and Adriyel 's eyes fell on his desk. He rubbed his chin, and stared forward as he tried to make sense of all he'd seen.

"She knew that you and the other sorcerers would be looking for it," Taryn added as he squeezed my shoulders. "We'll find another way. I'm sure the Oracle himself is trying to look as well."

Adriyel's head shot up suddenly. "Oracle?"

Taryn and I stared at him, but a look of realization crossed Jael's face.

Adriyel rose to his feet. His eyes, which were closing wearily a moment ago, were now wide again in excitement and surprise. "I believe part of the problem may be that I am not powerful enough to break past Raveena's shield. She has most likely put up a protective spell around her hiding place to prevent anyone from finding your voice, but there is only a certain amount of power that a spell like that should be able to withstand."

"So you're saying that an Oracle should have the power to penetrate this shield and find Nhanni's voice?" Taryn asked.

"An Oracle," Adriyel replied, turning to me. "Or…an Oracle's heir."

This suggestion caught me by surprise, but I remained silent while Taryn stared at Adriyel with his mouth open.

Adriyel sighed. "Relax, Taryn. Do not look at me like that-"

"Absolutely *out of the question*! We've known she's the Oracle's heir for less than an hour and you're planning on sending her to Raveena's home without protection?"

"Taryn-"

"Forget it!"

Jael came to my other side, putting his arm around me. "For once, we agree."

I think…I want to try.

Everyone's heads swiveled in my direction in the same second. I released a breath as Taryn shook his head. I know it's going to be dangerous…but if there's anything I can do to help I want to do it. Or at least try.

Taryn still wasn't convinced. "You don't understand, Nhanni. We have no way of knowing what the crystal will show you, or where it'll take you. It can sense who you are, make your worst fears become a reality; make you relive your most painful memories…there's a reason I myself haven't tried to find your voice. Yet."

I'll be fine. If things start to look bad you can just pull me out. I have nothing to lose by trying.

"Nhanni..." Jael said seriously. "Did you stop to think about what might happen if Raveena senses that you're there? Being the Oracle's heir, your aura's quite noticeable. If she knows we're getting closer to finding your voice, she'll find a way to make sure we *never* do."

We all sighed in unison, our gazes dropping while silent thoughts filled our minds. Adriyel's expression turned thoughtful, and I too considered what Taryn and Jael had said.

I know there are risks, I said at last. *But I still want to try.*

"Nhanni-"

I'll talk you through what's happening. The moment you think I've been there long enough, you can pull me out.

Adriyel looked as if he was considering. After a moment, he nodded. "She will be fine, Taryn. We will all be watching, and nothing can physically harm her in that dreamlike state."

I squeezed Taryn's hand, and Jael's arm tightened around my shoulders.

"Fine," he replied at last. His eyes locked on mine, and we both nodded. "Let's give it a try."

I crossed the room with Adriyel and stood beside his desk, Taryn and Jael supporting me on either side. I took a deep breath then reached my hand out and let my fingers gently brush the cold glass. Instantly, I was pulled into the vision, as quickly as it took for me to fall asleep. I could easily have mistaken the visions I was seeing as nothing more than broken flashes of a dream.

I was in Taryn's living room again.

Sunlight was streaming though the tall windows, and falling across the floors in long, golden streaks. I could see the dust drifting through the light. The room was filled with a quiet humming. It drew me towards the tall looking-glass against the wall, its surface shimmering in the evening light.

As my fingers touched the glass, it rippled like the surface of water, and I plunged forward into a liquid-ice ocean. Tiny bubbles caressed me as I fell, surrounding me and blurring my vision as I peered through the dark waters.

"Nhanni?" I recognized the voice…Taryn's.

It's cold, Taryn. And dark. I can't swim…the crystal knows I can't swim.

"It's not real, Nhanni. The crystal is testing you, to see if you can get past your fear. To see if you can overcome it."

I can't breathe.

"Yes you can. Concentrate...tell yourself that you can swim to the surface. Tell yourself that you can breathe, and you *can*. Focus."

Slowly, the water began refracting light from somewhere. I released the breath I'd been holding, bubbles escaped, and my vision dimmed. I was close to the surface now. I could see where the dim light was broken in rippling patterns, and I started to push myself up. I felt another pull, and I was wrenched out of the water and back through the surface of the mirror.

I coughed and gasped as I tumbled to the carpeted floor, even though I'd been able to breathe underwater just like Taryn said. I shivered in my soaked clothes, slowly pushing myself to my feet and taking in my surroundings. It was not Taryn's living room, but the same room I'd seen in my dreams before.

I think I'm there. I think...I'm in Raveena's house.

"Yes! Wonderful job, Nhanni. Now that you're there you should be able to sense your voice. Not only will you be drawn to its power as an Oracle, but it's *your* voice and will try to call you back so it can return to you."

I glanced around the room, and listened intently. The ominous silence left no sound. Just when I was about to give up, I heard a small voice; nothing more than a whisper, but I knew which direction it was coming from. I walked along the wall, looking at each seemingly ordinary object as I passed. It was very likely that Raveena would not keep such useless things unless they carried magic.

There were shelves piled with old books, their bindings falling apart and their covers coated in a thin layer of dust. The strange objects cluttered the large dining table, pushed up against the wall in the corner of the room. I scanned the objects quickly: a pure white feather, a rusted dagger, a crystal amulet, piles of books, and papers covered in elegant script.

I turned abruptly when the voices grew louder, and I felt drawn towards the intense heat of the flames dancing in the tall fireplace. I watched the tendrils wave from side to side, violet flames rather than orange. Moving shapes appeared as the voices rang in my ears.

Down the hall, a door closed, pulling me out of my trance. I heard light footsteps growing louder, drawing closer.

It's Raveena!

"What?"

Give me a moment! I nearly have it!

I could hear Taryn's muffled protests as I moved to the other side of the fireplace, quickly sifting through the thick volumes resting on a shelf. The footsteps sounded as though they were right next to me now, and I knew Raveena was about to enter.

"Nhanni!"

I was wrenched from the dream. Jael's arms held me upright as I staggered away from the crystal.

"Are you alright?" Adriyel and Taryn asked me, nearly in unison.

I buried my face in Jael's shirt to hide the angry tears that stung my eyes. I'd been so close, and couldn't help but blame them for pulling me back before I'd found my voice. But countering this anger was gratitude; I was so afraid at the thought of Raveena finding me that the safety of Adriyel's office was welcome. After a moment of silence, I let out a long sigh. Now, all I could feel was disappointment in myself. *I'm sorry, Adriyel. I couldn't find it...my voice is still hidden.*

Chapter twenty one

Raveena

"Looks like I didn't have to summon you again," I said, with a grin to myself. "You came back all on your own."

I turned, and he lifted a hooded head, only enough for me to see the slow movement of his mouth as he spoke. "*Someone* had to stop you."

"Stop me?"

"Do not *mock* me, Raveena. I am the Oracle. Don't you know I can read your intentions as plainly as an open book?"

I grit my teeth and paced away from him, watching him in the seven-foot mirrors lining the hall. "I suppose I should have suspected you would have such power, but I am still surprised. So you've realized what I am planning, have you?"

"It is futile. The prophecy refers to the wielder of that stone and no one else. *Dust of the Stars* is destined for the royal sorcerer. I have only returned because it seems you did not want to give up, even though I have already explained that it is impossible for you to get what you wish. Even if you obtain the power, it will not fall under your command. It will resist."

He spoke of magic as if it was alive. "I understand perfectly, Oracle. Once he is on the throne, the boy will have great power. But if I can control the boy, I can control his magic, and therefore the entire kingdom."

"You cannot *control* him, Raveena, that is *dark magic*! It is forbidden!" The Oracle roared.

"I have never had a problem using such magic to get what I want, although there is a risk of being found out and arrested by Adriyel and the Army, despite my threats to destroy that girl's voice, her magic, and her very life in the process. Fortunately for me though, I will not have to manipulate the boy at all."

"Fool. He will not come willingly," the Oracle replied.

"Are you certain?"

"I do not know how well you know him, Raveena, but he has changed. *That* much is certain. Unlike you, he will not resort to dark magic to gain power. The prophecy is no longer all that he cares about."

"You speak of him as if you know him, Oracle."

He fell silent, and my pressed lips turned into a grin as I met his gaze. "I suppose it only makes sense for you to watch him closely, as he is the subject of your prophecy."

"Indeed, I *have* been near Adriyel and his students. Although the boy cannot be harmed, the other apprentices are in danger from other sorcerers all the time."

I sighed to myself, turning away again so that he could not see my frustration. With the Oracle near The Academy, it would be difficult to make any move toward the boy, who was surely watched closely by Adriyel as well. Not to mention the fact that he seemed to be constantly surrounded by groups of friends. Something clicked in my head, after a moment. I stopped pacing. The boy certainly knew the other students, and could be threatened to do as I wished.

"Do not even *think* about it."

I glared in the Oracle's direction, more annoyed than angry that he could tell exactly what I was planning. "It won't matter if you are there, Oracle. The human heart is weak. Jael will join me if he knows the people he cares about are in danger, and the prophecy will indeed come true."

"You cannot threaten anyone to get to Jael," he replied, his voice surprisingly calm.

He stared me down, the small reflection of light in his eyes sent a shiver up my spine. He did not raise his face into the light, but I could hear the faint sound as he released a long breath. "I have kept the truth from everyone long enough."

I spun away from the mirror, trying to keep my face calm as I faced him. "*What truth?*"

"The prophecy refers to the sorcerer who will wield *Dust of the stars*, the precious stone."

"Yes, I know. The medallion that the boy wears."

The Oracle grinned, and I could feel my eyes widen in horror. "Unfortunately for you…" he replied, his smile spreading. "…the boy's medallion is not *Dust of the stars.*"

"What?"

"The true stone remains protected, as well as its holder."

"You *tricked* me!" I shrieked, my hand raising automatically as I prepared to fight him. After a moment, I sighed and held back my anger. Even *I* didn't stand a chance against an Oracle.

"I had to keep the stone's true wielder safe from you, Raveena. Your efforts are in vain, as I have said many times. The prophecy will come true, and you will be powerless to stop it."

"How *dare-*"

His ghostly laughter interrupted me, and I stood frozen as he disappeared before my eyes. In the fireplace, the bright violet flames flickered and died.

"Treacherous fool," I muttered, clenching my fist together as if crushing that little girl's life. "He has *no idea* who he's dealing with…"

Chapter twenty two

Nhanni

Flakes, snowflakes, fell like dust scattered through shades of light, cascading across my otherwise empty vision. Slowly, like silver droplets of water rising from the darkness of the ocean's consciousness, wonders and ideas rising up from what was once thought to be an empty void. Sweet sorrows and soft tortures coming to light beneath the ripples above, glistening with golden harmony.

All above was distorted light, a paradise twisted, moved, and invisible to eyes glancing upward. Small, tentative, hands reach into oblivion, risking the safety of their haven to leap into their dreams of an eclipsed paradise.

All along they knew what it was worth to succeed, to arrive, and also what was lost along the way. There is only the struggle to survive and the chances taken to be better. There are only the barely audible moans of those too frightened to seek, too ashamed to escape the darkness of their drowning dreams.

There is only an endless eternity, a moment of truth everlasting to those who wait, to those who can't even dream a dream or imagine a hope. All the years spent wishing and hours past waiting drop into a vast sea, like the remains of a ship lost on its way home. There is only a voyage fulfilled or tried, only a journey completed or forgotten. There is only time, endless time that never vanishes, slows, or changes victims. There is only time, waiting for us to leap, and wondering if we are even prepared.

The soft moans reach the surface only to scatter in small droplets, like fireworks exploding before tortured eyes. The only sound is the catastrophic mayhem, drowned in the magnificent kaleidoscope of the light's death. Those tortured eyes can only see the beauty in death. They can only watch with memorised hopes, oblivious to the frightened howls from below.

All the world is an empty voice, an open space that lies between the safe and the brave. Only a void echoing with cries of joy and despair. Only a long forgotten dream, unachieved by the ones who made it up. There is only a voice in the darkness to guide us, a mirrored self, a reflection of a personality yet to come.

There is only the image of our consciousness brought to life, pleading for our first steps. Torturing us to escape ourselves, and hoping we will win against the forces dragging us behind. Dragging us like legs, weary and worn from years of travel through the thick, slimy mud clinging to our boots. We are dragged through. We are dragged until we finally take the courage to remove the boots we desperately cling to, and run through the mud with bare, vulnerable feet.

It felt like I'd been sitting, staring at the pages of my journal, for hours. I ached all over from sitting in the old, wooden chair. Nearly everything in The Academy was ancient and boring, but familiar. I knew the scent of incense so well, I would be able to smell it and know right away that Adriyel was at his desk reading, enveloped in the relaxing scents which allowed him to forget the outside world for a while. Right now, it hovered around me like a storm cloud, the sweet scent drifting down on me like light mist. Everything in the school creaked; the floors, the shelves, the chairs, the doors…ensuring that, even during the night, these halls never fell into complete silence.

I was unprepared to leave this life behind…or this home. I glanced at Jael sitting at his desk, fumbling with the large medallion around his neck. Adriyel sat at the front of the room, sighing to himself every now and then. His feet were propped up on a shelf and he was slowly flipping through the pages of what appeared to be an old spellbook, his rectangular glasses on the tip of his nose. Taryn was sprawled across the stone bench by the window, staring intently at the road. He could have been mistaken for a statue, until he groaned again and let his head fall back.

"Time will pass more slowly the more you wait," Adriyel muttered.

"It's been *three* days…what on earth is taking Rowyn so long?"

"You forget that Windylow is far away, Taryn. It will be longer than three days before he arrives; it will take him three days just to travel from the border of Arheynia. He probably had to prepare himself for life in the palace, as well," Adriyel pointed out, with a quick glance at me. "It will be a big change, for *all* of us."

I sighed in defeat and put my journal away, resting my head in my hands.

Jael glanced up. "I wonder why the Oracle hasn't appeared."

Adriyel cocked his eyebrow.

"I mean there can only be *one* real Oracle at a time, right? So I just don't understand why he hasn't shown himself. He must have known Nhanni would be his successor long before *we* figured it out."

Adriyel nodded. "You are right. Not only should he be here to make Nhanni his apprentice, but he should be extremely protective of her as his only possible heir."

"Okay..." Jael said, confused. "Then why don't you sound surprised?"

"Because even though the Oracle has not shown himself, that does not mean he is not already here. It is possible that he has been here ever since Nhanni first entered The Academy, keeping an eye on her from close by. He could very well be one of the staff, or even a *student*."

A student? I asked in surprise. That would make him the same age as us. How is that even possible?

Adriyel chuckled softly. "Nhanni...he is an *Oracle*. He can quite easily keep himself young for a hundred years if he wants to. He can appear any age, at any time; he could be a small child or an old man. That is why no one knows who he really is; whenever he shows himself, he can take a different form."

"Why would he do that... stay young forever?" Jael asked.

Adriyel cocked his head in my direction. "He has been waiting for *her*. His only heir."

"Oh," Jael looked away, deep in thought again. "I wonder if it's someone we know. Morahn, Garett...even *Gabe*."

Taryn snorted at this idea.

"You have not heard?" Adriyel asked Jael, his eyes widening. " I am sorry that you have to hear this from me, but Gabe has given up magic and left The Academy. He is attending a mortal school now."

I saw Jael grin to himself.

Taryn groaned again. "We can't be here where it's not safe. Let's just go to the palace and meet Nhanni's father *there*."

Adriyel sighed and tossed the spellbook he was trying to read onto his desk. "I think you may be right, Taryn. The only person powerful enough to protect Nhanni is the other Oracle, and since he refuses to reveal his identity, the only place she is safe is within the boundaries of the palace."

"Is it really safe enough? Can't the boundaries be broken?" Jael asked.

"No," Taryn replied, looking away from the window. "The Oracle himself put up that boundary. Only he or Nhanni would ever be able to break it."

"That's a relief," Jael said, releasing a breath. The fire flickered ominously as Adriyel, Taryn, and I echoed his sigh.

Adriyel stood up from his desk. "This is taking too long. Prepare to leave, you three. We must get to the palace before anyone tries to come after you, Nhanni."

We nodded, and gratefully stood after sitting and waiting for such a long time.

"I'll send a messenger for Rowyn. He's on the move, and we have to reach him as soon as possible," Taryn offered, stepping out the door and calling one of the workers.

Taryn spoke quietly to him for several minutes. Though his voice was hushed, I could hear a hint of urgency. He came back inside the ballroom when the messenger's rapid footsteps could be heard retreating down the hall. I sighed, grabbing my bag off my desk and slinging it over my shoulder as Jael came up beside me. He glanced at Taryn's and Adriyel's turned backs before leaning forward for a kiss.

Taryn spun around, having noticed Jael's arm circling me. "Don't even *think* about it."

"But, how did you even know I was going to-"

"Oh please, like it wasn't *obvious*…"

"Enough, you two. We do not need this right now." Adriyel sighed, shoving old spellbooks into a giant bag.

I couldn't help but chuckle as I watched. That's Adriyel's idea of packing for you.

Taryn and Jael continued to glare at each other, eyes narrow and fists clenched.

Please guys. Not now.

There was another long silence. Jael's gaze fell, and his expression turned thoughtful again.

"Taryn's right," he finally said, looking at me sadly. "All of this is *my* fault."

You shouldn't blame yourself. This is as much my fault as it is yours, I told him and gently squeezed his hand.

"If it weren't for the prophecy-"

"The prophecy hardly even matters anymore," Adriyel said suddenly.

All three of us looked at him.

"People will no longer be after you to threaten *Jael*, Nhanni," he explained. "Think about it. Who is the most powerful sorcerer in Arheynia right now; more powerful than Jael and *me* as well?"

"The Oracle, of course," Jael replied.

"One downside to being an Oracle; there is only *one* heir. If an Oracle's heir dies, it can be a very long time before another appears. The Oracle that was born before you, Nhanni, was killed, and that is why the present Oracle has been waiting for you so long."

Taryn nodded. "Which makes Nhanni the Oracle's only weakness."

"And threatening an Oracle can get someone almost *anything* they want. It gives one immense power. Which means…as soon as people find out who Nhanni is, Jael and the prophecy will very likely be completely forgotten."

"I don't understand…" Jael murmured. "If an Oracle's power is as great as you say, couldn't Nhanni easily defeat anyone who comes after her?"

"She is still learning, don't forget. It doesn't help that her voice was stolen either. And Nhanni does not technically become the next Oracle until the current one bestows her with her true name. Her name of power."

"That's right…a name of power will unlock one's true potential."

Adriyel nodded, finished packing his bag, and swung the enormous load onto his back. "I am ready. Get your things together, all of you."

I moved sluggishly towards the door, but Taryn stepped in front of me. "I'll get your bag from your room, Nhanni. You should stay here with Adriyel, where you're safe."

I nodded in agreement, and he and Jael turned to leave.

As I turned back, I noticed my journal lying on my desk. A strange violet light reflected off its cover. I was almost positive I'd packed it in my bag earlier.

That's weird…I said to myself as I reached for it.

Adriyel glanced in my direction, and a gasp escaped his lips when he noticed the journal. "That aura…that's-! Nhanni, don't touch-!"

I had already grabbed it, and instantly it evaporated into powdery purple light. I coughed. The aura seemed to melt into my body, freezing every muscle, and every breath. I couldn't move, and could barely breathe. I fell to the floor, coughing and gasping for air.

"Nhanni!" Taryn and Jael called in unison, running to me. All three of them were beside me, but the thoughts in my mind were so chaotic I was unable to tell them anything. I felt caught in a snowstorm, frozen down to my bones and drowning in my own breath. I felt like I was being drained somehow, as if the very warmth, the very *life*, was being sucked out of me.

"This is bad…very, very bad!" Adriyel said over and over, touching my forehead and muttering spells under his breath.

Jael looked horrified. "Nhanni!"

"There is no point. She cannot move or speak."

"What's wrong with her?"

"This is *Adficio Vis Vires*, a forbidden spell."

Taryn's eyes widened. "A *forbidden* spell? You mean-?"

"A curse."

"What's happening to her?" Jael asked.

Adriyel shook his head in disbelief. "Someone is stealing her magic, sucking it right out of her; whoever it is must have found out she is the next Oracle. There is no other explanation for such ominous sorcery. The curse is designed so that it is impossible to stop it, even for Nhanni. It is useless."

Jael, with his face drained, looked like a ghost."There's nothing we can do? What if we find whoever is doing this?"

Adriyel sighed loudly, pondering the idea a moment. There was a long silence before he glanced up, his face unusually hard. "This is ancient magic…quite powerful, I might add. And I would recognize that aura anywhere. There is only *one* sorceress who could be doing this."

"Who?"

Adriyel and Taryn exchanged a worried glance.

"*Raveena*," Taryn hissed angrily.

Chapter twenty three

Jael

"Where are you *going*?" Taryn demanded, as he motioned to a different hallway. "The healer is *this* way."

"I know!" I replied roughly. "I don't usually get lost, but I'm just *slightly* panicky right now!"

Taryn sighed, nodding as he speed-walked down the hallway. I grunted as I carried Nhanni after him.

"Here it is."

We entered a brightly lit room, where the healer was arranging different spells in a small cupboard before she noticed us. "Oh my…*Nhanni* again?"

"She's been cursed," I explained, setting Nhanni down. "*Vis Vires*. Please, see what you can do."

"Not much, I'm afraid," the woman replied. She glanced at Nhanni with a tight frown. "How long has she been unconscious?"

"I…I don't know," I stuttered, blinking when my eyes tried to fill with moisture.

Taryn just stared at Nhanni, his face hard as stone.

"I will have to get another dose. Wait here."

The healer shoved a small bottle into Taryn's hand. "Sprinkle this over her eyes. I'll be back shortly."

She left in a hurry. Taryn tried to remove the lid, his fingers fumbling as he rushed. He emptied what appeared to be gold powder into his hand, and he gently sprinkled it over Nhanni's eyes. The powder drifted down, like millions of tiny stars, then it slowly absorbed into her body. We sat, waiting impatiently as her pale aura flickered like a dying flame.

"Nothing's happening!" I panicked again.

Taryn sighed heavily and motioned for me to calm down. "Is she coming?"

I peered down the hall, but didn't see any sign of the healer. "No."

"Alright. Stay there and tell me if you see or hear anything."

I nodded, watching intently as he raised his hands above Nhanni and took another deep breath. "What are you going to do?"

"I'm going to counter the spell. It's the only way. I can't lift the curse, but maybe I can at least wake her up."

"You mean there's a spell to reverse it?" I asked as his aura appeared.

"Did you *ever* pay attention in class? *Every* spell has an opposite; a reverse."

"Why didn't Adriyel use it, then?"

Taryn sighed heavily. "Because in order to counter it, he has to be stronger than whoever cursed her. In this case…Raveena."

"And you think *you* are?" I glanced down the hall once again and shook my head. "You must be out of your *mind*."

"I'm desperate."

After a moment of silence, I nodded in agreement. "Alright. Then at least take this." I quickly pulled the medallion over my head, handing it to Taryn. "That stone holds power."

"The prophecy-"

"Who *cares*? You're wasting time!"

Taryn quickly pulled the medallion over his head with a nod, raising his hands and closing his eyes again.

"Don't be alarmed. This is a long spell, and it will take a while to complete."

I stood frozen.

"*Exsuscito*," Taryn mumbled softly, his hands trembling.

I recognized that word; 'Awake'.

"*Reneo in textus veritas*

In labyrinthus de is milliare fila," Taryn recited, in a voice so deep and demanding it was hard to believe it belonged to him. He spoke each word with such weight, such intensity. It raised goose bumps along my arms.

The medallion began to glow with light as I watched.

"*Excido etiam vos inretio*

Et odeo eam citra timor."

The bright torches around us started to twist and flicker, and on the other side of the window the wind howled.

"Taryn…" I said in a quaking voice, but he continued to recite the spell.

"Disparo praestrigia ex vos oculos
Quo spectrum reside sculptilis in decipio."

The medallion's light faded and Taryn squeezed his eyes shut, looking as if he was in pain.

"Taryn!" I said, and quickly stood on the other side of Nhanni, placing my hands in his open palms. "Keep going. Channel my power."

I closed my eyes, and Taryn finished the spell.

"Exsuscito ex impervious duditare
Et pando vos oculos ex somnia de nunquam pervigilia."

I opened my eyes, hesitantly relaxing and letting my magic fade. I sighed in relief as the wind and flickering lights finally died down. Taryn turned towards me with a small smile, then released my hands and gently touched Nhanni's forehead.

"Exsuscito," he whispered softly.

Almost immediately, her eyes opened.

"Incredible…" I said in surprise, astonished by the strength of Taryn's power . "She's awake!"

Nhanni squinted into the dim light as her eyes focused, slowly turning her head to the side. *Taryn? Jael?*

"Good," said Taryn. "So you still have enough magic to use your *Mens Mentis*."

Yeah, but just barely. It's hard now.

"I know. You'll be fine soon. Adriyel summoned the Royal Army and went after Raveena."

My gaze had slowly traveled to the floor, staring at nothing as I once again fell deep into the thought. "He won't find her. *No one will…*" I said quietly to myself.

"What?" Taryn asked, cocking his eyebrow.

I locked eyes with him, communicating my determination without words. "Stay here with Nhanni!"

Jael? Nhanni said worriedly as I bolted out the door.

Taryn was right behind me. "Where are you going?"

"I'm going to make things right."

"What? How are you going to-?"

"Trust me, Taryn. A lot of this is my fault, and I have to fix it."

He stared with a look of disbelief, and for a long time, we were both silent.

Taryn was the first to speak. "You have to come back, Jael."

My mouth popped open. "*What?*"

"Nhanni needs you. She *loves* you, and it will break her heart if you don't come back."

I couldn't summon a reply and his face fell, his familiar smile pressing into a tight frown. He took a deep breath as his expression abruptly turned sad. It was the first time I'd ever seen him this way. "You have no idea…how lucky you are."

I stared at him in surprise for a moment longer, before I understood. "Her dream…" I said, nodding my head guiltily. "You thought it was talking about *you*."

Taryn eyed the door nervously, and motioned for me to be silent. "*No one* can know."

"Nhanni is going to figure it out anyway, Taryn. No, you have to tell her."

Now his hard expression abruptly turned shocked. "You want me to-? *Why*?"

I let out a huge sigh, trying to understand it myself.

"Because you've been her best friend since she entered The Academy." I tried my best to smile. "I have to accept that you will always be a big part of her life, and it will hurt her just as much if she loses *you*."

After a moment, Taryn finally returned my smile, his expression unusually soft. "Thank you, Jael. I admit…I was wrong about you."

I nodded in thanks. When he didn't say anything else, I turned to leave.

"Jael-!" Taryn began.

I turned back. His hard, but slightly worried, expression softened into a grin as he removed the medallion and tossed it to me. I caught it reflexively, but wrinkled my brow to show I was confused.

His grin spread. "Just don't do anything *stupid*."

My smile returned, and I quickly retreated down the corridor as I pulled the medallion over my head. "Not making any promises, Taryn."

*****

I stood outside the door for a long time, breathing deeply, staring at the worn doorknocker. Eventually I told myself I would never be ready, and quickly stepped inside the small cottage. I came down the hall, turned the corner, and there she stood, holding her long elegant fingers towards the flickering violet flames.

"Jael…what a wonderful surprise."

I grit my teeth as she turned around, and I stepped up to her. "You *cursed* her-!"

"I had my reasons."

"Break the spell *at once!*"

"I'm afraid it's already complete. The majority of that girl's powers are sealed, and only *I* know where. If that stupid boy hadn't counter-cursed it, she wouldn't have any power at all."
She sighed and flicked her long dark hair over her shoulder.
"Unfortunately, some magic has stayed with her. That girl just *refuses* to go down, no matter what I try."

"Why are you doing this?"

"Revenge. The Oracle was foolish enough to get on my bad side."

I just cocked my eyebrow.

"The prophecy does not speak of you, Jael. That medallion of yours holds power, but it is a fake."

"What?"

"Yes, he has been tricking me this entire time to protect the true wielder of the stone. And now that I have his only heir's power sealed, he will do anything to have me break it. Even help get me my rightful place on the throne."

It grew too difficult for me to keep my composure, and I stormed towards her again. "Is that why you've been pushing me about the prophecy so much? You thought that I would just *let* you control me once I was the king's sorcerer?"

"Darling-"

"Don't you *dare* 'darling' me! Do you even *hear* yourself? If I'd have known what you were planning-"

"What?" she asked with a grin, shrugging her shoulders. "What would you have done? I'm your *mother*."

"That means *nothing* to me!" I roared, and quickly stepped away from her. She reached for my arm. "Not anymore."

She took a slow, calming breath as she dropped her arm slowly back to her side. Violet flames flickered at the tips of her hair, and I could see the heat rising to her cheeks. "I was afraid that it would come to this...don't make me *force* you to help me."

"There's absolutely *nothing* you can do to force me. I'm telling Adriyel the truth. I may not be the sorcerer from the prophecy, and I may not be powerful enough to beat you, but Adriyel *is*. And so is Taryn…I've seen it with my own eyes."

"Are you sure there's nothing I can do to force you?" she asked, pouting her lip. "Not even…kill that girl you love?"

I froze instantly. "How-?"

"Oh please, Jael. I've known for months that you've had a little crush on her. The rumors buzzing through the school, however, seemed to suggest that it was much more than that."

"Don't you *dare* harm her!"

"If you agree, then I won't have to. As long as her voice and her magic remain sealed, her life is in my hands. You are going to do exactly what I say…or she will die."

I clenched my fist together tightly, making her grin in triumph.

"Make your choice, son."

"Don't call me that!"

"Why ever not?"

"You really expect me to believe that I'm *your* son? It can't just be a coincidence that I was the original subject of the prophecy, the wielder of the stone you were constantly searching for."

"No, it wasn't. See, the Oracle knew that I would come after Adriyel's apprentice as soon as I found out who it was," Raveena explained.

"He did not invent the prophecy, but he lied about the medallion so that I would believe it was talking about *you*. He wanted to protect the true wielder of *Dust of the stars*."

She turned away from me, staring intently at the tall mirrors that reflected the flames in the fireplace.

"Who?" I asked after a moment.

She sighed heavily. "I haven't figured that out, yet. I have, however, begun to suspect the girl's friend. From what I've heard, and from what you've just told me, his power is much too extraordinary for just *any* student."

"Taryn...*of course*."

There was a long silence as the fire flickered ominously, violet tendrils spinning out in an explosion of sparks. I knew the choice I had to make, and I knew I would regret confronting Raveena for the rest of my life.

"You have to give me your word you will not harm Taryn or Nhanni."

Her eyes flashed with excitement as she spun back around. "Are you accepting then, son? Will you really help *me* get what I want just to save that girl's life?"

"Yes."

Her grin reappeared.

I took a deep breath, holding my chin high and refusing to give her the satisfaction of seeing my fear show. "What are you going to make me do?"

Chapter twenty four

Nhanni

I sighed and absentmindedly flipped through the dusty pages of one of Adriyel's spellbooks. Originally, I was passing time, wondering why the flipping of worn pages was so calming to me, but now I knew twice as many spells as before. It bothered me that I couldn't even use any of them, as long as Raveena had most of my powers sealed and managed to stay hidden from the king's sorcerers. I could use my *Mens Mentis* to communicate, but that was mostly it.

I was still having dreams though.

Last night, I dreamt I was standing across the long living room from Raveena, the dark, violet flames casting ominous reflections in the giant mirrors, and Jael was standing next to *her* instead of me.

I knew *that* couldn't be good.

I glanced at my journal, then shook my head. It was silly to write anything at a time like this. I turned back to the spellbook:

Infirmitas and *Novus*: the spells for weakening and strengthening.

Solum: the spell for earth.

Aeris: the spell for air

Aqua: the spell for water.

On and on I read, until I couldn't take it anymore. I stood up from my bed and, even though I knew it was late, left my room and headed towards Adriyel's office. It was pitch black. The faint glow of the lamps lit my way as I rounded the huge building, pulling down the hood of my thick cloak. The fresh air and quiet noise of crickets was peaceful, but I noticed that the breeze was chilly. I stopped, shivering, and was about to go back inside when I noticed a familiar figure retreating down the stone path.

I ran after him. *Jael?*

He froze and whirled quickly around to face me, surprised, then his expression became hard.

I smiled and placed a hand on his shoulder. *Taryn and I were worried. Why didn't you come to find me when you got back?*

He shrugged my hand off without meeting my gaze, stepping away with an absent, thoughtful look. It was only then that I noticed the large bag he was carrying, as well as the thick cloak slung carelessly over his shoulders. *Jael? Are you…going somewhere?*

His expression turned stone cold. "I'm leaving The Academy, Nhanni."

W…what?

"I'm leaving. And, I'm not coming back."

I stood staring at him silently for a moment, running through the words in my head to convince myself that I'd heard right. *Why?*

"The prophecy was wrong. I was never destined to be the king's sorcerer, it's someone else," he explained.

I stepped up to him again, shaking my head to show I was confused. I don't understand. That's not any reason for you to leave.

"Don't you get it? I don't have any reason to *stay* anymore! My entire life I've been waiting to take my place on the throne, and now it belongs to someone else!"

What brought on this? I asked, surprised by his anger. Taryn told me that you left to stop Raveena.

He stared at me a long time, and there was something about his eyes. He was regarding me with such emptiness, such coldness, but there was hidden sadness there as well. "I did see her, Nhanni, but it had nothing to do with the curse. She's been planning all along for me to take the throne, and with you under her curse the Oracle will give her anything she wants."

This can't be happening, I said softly, before taking a breath, preparing myself for the worst. Are you...are you working with Raveena?

His eyes were ice cold now; any light that had once shone there was now gone. "Worse. She's my mother."

I couldn't bring myself to say anything.

I couldn't even think. So I just stood there with my mouth sealed shut, unable to look away. There was nothing but truth in his gaze, no matter how hard I looked.

This is impossible, I finally began. I turned away, looking anywhere but at him. How can this be? I was beginning to think that you were the Oracle.

He laughed at the idea.

At that moment, I knew there was something seriously wrong with Jael. There was absolutely *nothing* in him. No kindness, no worry, no regret, no feelings at all.

I turned back. What happened to you? I asked, so faintly in my mind I'd be surprised if he heard.

"Nothing."

No, it can't be nothing! Raveena must be controlling you! But that means...did you tell her your true name?!

His face only hardened. "No."

I stepped towards him again, grabbing his hand. What have you done? You have to let me release you from her spell! You can't let her control you!

"I'm not being controlled!" he yelled, yanking his arm away. "I wanted this! I've been working with Ravenna willingly this entire time!"

Why? Tears streamed down my face, as I hugged my shoulders and shivered each time the sharp wind ripped through me.

Jael took no notice. "Power. I want my rightful place on the throne…the place that should've been my mother's to begin with. The Oracle had no right to trick us."

You're lying!

"Open your eyes, Nhanni! Can't you see that this has all been a plan? Right from the very beginning?"

I stared, my words stopped in their tracks as I thought back to my first class with him. And then, I thought back even further, and the pieces all fell into place as if I'd turned to the last page of a mystery.

"You were meant to lose your voice, enter The Academy, and become Adriyel's apprentice."

I shook my head.

"You were meant to choose me as your partner, to fall in love with me."

I shook my head harder.

"It was all part of the plan, for me to get close to you and earn your trust." Jael stepped up to me, leaning forward so that his face was inches from mine. "I never loved you."

There was a long, deafening silence. Even the crickets and howling wind seemed to have quieted. I only whimpered. My tears grew hot, stinging my cheeks against the chill of the air. Then, my whimpers became sobs.

Jael didn't speak. He didn't even seem to care. He simply spun around, and strode defiantly into the darkness.

Jael!

He was already gone, and I managed to shuffle across the path to a bench. I lowered myself onto the cold stone, curling into a ball. I stayed there for what felt like an eternity, shivering and sobbing. I felt like the earth was collapsing under me, like the sky was raining down on me and each drop was a thousand-ton weight.

And then, of course, it started raining for real.

I stopped crying and lay there, letting the water soak me right through my clothes.

I felt empty now. I did not even have the strength to shiver anymore.I closed my eyes, and was just falling asleep when I heard footsteps coming down the stone path. I didn't open my eyes as the footfall stopped beside me. Familiar arms scooped me up.

"Nhanni…" his velvet voice whispered. "I'm so sorry."

Taryn–

"Shhh…just sleep." He was carrying me back inside, and I sighed as the warmth surrounded me.

Taryn…you must be getting tired of saving me.

Though my eyes weren't open, I could tell he was grinning. "*Someone* has to."

Chapter twenty five

Jael

I came up the steps to the cottage, feeling like my feet weighed a hundred pounds. Every part of me, from my skin down to my bones, felt numb, as if I'd lost all feeling in every fiber of my being. I wore no expression at all, my mind was blank.

With a heavy sigh, I stepped inside, dropping my enormous bag on the floor before turning the corner. Mother was there, staring at the flickering surface of a seven-foot mirror in the dim light.

My eyes began to water at what I saw.

Raveena was holding her hand towards the glass, her forehead wrinkled in concentration as she watched the images beginning to form beneath the smooth surface. I could plainly see that it was Taryn and Nhanni, in what appeared to be her room at The Academy. They had their arms around each other and Nhanni was sobbing into his shoulder, her face hidden from view but her body shaking noticeably.

I felt my chest tighten, as if at any moment, without warning, it would suddenly burst.

"Shhh…" was all Taryn said, stroking her hair softly.

I can't begin to describe how hard it was to see her like this…with *him*, almost as hard as it was to accept that it was *my* fault. We watched a while longer, and Nhanni didn't stop crying even after the image in the mirror slowly faded.

Raveena turned towards me, her hand falling gracefully back to her side. She didn't seem fazed by my expression, she didn't seem to even care how much this hurt me.

And *Nhanni*.

I knew, then and there, I was going to make her pay for making me do the very thing Taryn had warned me not to do. I couldn't stand the fact that Nhanni was under the impression I'd betrayed her, and *used* her; anger began boiling over inside me just thinking about it.

I stared coldly at Raveena and I clenched my fist, resisting the urge to smash her thin, delicate nose.

Her vibrant red lips pulled up into a grin. "Well done, Jael."

Chapter twenty six

Nhanni

Cold bites with the jagged, pointed teeth of a tiger, cutting with the piercing numbness of winter ripping through layers of coats and scarves. Just as betrayal pierces deeper than any wound, hurts us more with its sudden and shaking revelations. Betrayal is the cold sting of winter on a predicted sunny forecast, when I boldly strode from the safe shelter of my home in nothing more than a light sundress, trusting what I thought to be true, only to be bitten by an unpredicted frost.

I thought it was safe for me to let my guard down. I thought that, just once, my instincts were right, that there was such a thing as a pure, untainted heart. I had truly believed in love, but it was love from which the betrayal came.

I had believed in trust.

I thought that the paradise slowly taking shape before me was truly real, that it wasn't just an illusion or the sweet invention of my speechless hope.

I thought my heart's words and desires had come to be without my voice, but my silence was never to be more than that.

Silence.

It was foolish of me to think it could be more.

I was, and would forever be, silence, both in voice and presence. I couldn't truly be heard by anyone, the world didn't care about anything but words. Empty words, empty promises echoed through the dim, tranquil night, but never acted upon. Words are nothing, sad, pathetic, and worthless both on paper and tongues.

Silence matters.

Because when the world is silent, our hearts can speak. They can be heard, once the drowning chaos of the world is tuned down, and we listen...and act.

Silence matters, because when there is no room to speak...there is room to move. To release muscles and bones sighing with stiff relief, as they shift from the painful position in which they had posed for so long.

I stopped, and dropped my pen with a sigh.

Taryn, who I thought was asleep in the small chair by my desk, lifted his head and looked at me. I couldn't bring myself to write anymore. Now *I* was the one pacing back and forth across my room. I'd been annoyed with Adriyel earlier, but I was starting to understand why he found it hard to sit still.

We can't just sit around The Academy while Adriyel's out looking for Raveena. We should be trying to help.

"I hate to tell you, Nhanni, but as the new Oracle you have to keep a low profile. The fewer people who know about you, the better. Why do you think the Oracle never really shows himself, and wears a cloak whenever he *does*?"

I sighed again, my paces speeding up. Yeah, I know. But-

"*And*," Taryn put in, with a sad smile. "You wouldn't be searching for Raveena. You'd be searching for *Jael*."

It's the same, anyways. We have to stop her from gaining control of the kingdom.

Taryn slowly rose to his feet, taking my shoulders so that I would stand still and face him. "She already has gained control...over Jael."

How do we even know he was being controlled? He sounded pretty convincing to me.

"I don't know, but that's the only explanation I can come up with."

I finally met his gaze, and his hands fell. "She must have control over him, or she must have threatened him in some way. It just doesn't make sense. The Jael I know would never work with Raveena…even if she is his *mother*."

My eyes fell away again. I know you're trying to make me feel better, Taryn. But the point is, he isn't the Jael we knew. He had us all fooled. He deliberately used his talents….his charms against us. I squeezed my eyes shut. Me most of all.

"Don't ever think that! Not for a second!" Taryn pulled me into his arms, and I didn't resist. He took a deep breath and began stroking my hair, remembering the calming effect it has over me. "We have to stop Raveena."

How? I managed.

There was a knock at the door, and Taryn stepped into the hall where a messenger was waiting. I could only make out faint mumbling.

"I see," Taryn replied, turned away so that I could not see his face.

What?

He listened for a few more seconds, nodding and saying "I will", before passing the messenger another piece of paper.
He waited, said "Yes, thank you.", then shut the door behind him as he came back inside.

What did he say?

"It was a message from Adriyel. They still haven't been able to find her. They used tracking spells, but Raveena's smart. She countered them and led The Army down two false trails already."

Oh great.

"There's something else. Come on." Taryn took my hand, and quickly pulled me out of my room and down the hall.

Where are we going?

He didn't answer. He led me down winding stairwells and hallways until we came out in front of the school, hitting a wall of cool air as we stepped outside. I saw that a carriage was waiting.

Taryn?

He turned to face me, releasing a breath and letting his shoulders fall. "I know where she is, and she has to be stopped. She's been keeping your voice hidden, threatening you to get to us, for too long. It's the only way, Nhanni."

Only way? You know that's crazy, Taryn! The only way to stop Raveena is to surrender and give her what she wants!

He didn't blink before replying. "That's what I'm doing. Giving her what she wants."

I stared. *But...Raveena wants the* throne. *She wants to lure the Oracle out of hiding, but no one knows where he-*

I stopped abruptly.

Taryn and I held each other's gaze for a moment, and suddenly, I knew. His expression suggested that the thought that had crossed my mind had been spot on.

Wait...

The corner of his mouth turned up into a smile. "I'm so sorry, Nhanni, for keeping the truth from you all this time."

My eyes widened. *You're-*

"An Oracle," he said, his fingers lightly brushing my cheek. "Just like *you*."

I could only stare.

He grinned. "Everything makes a *lot* more sense now, doesn't it?"

*Adriyel was right...*I said, trying to sound calm. *You've been watching me this whole time. My entire life.*

"Like I always say, *someone* had to keep you safe."

Does Adriyel-?

"No. You are the first person I have told. Ever."

I pulled away from him, almost losing my balance a few times as I stumbled down the path.

Taryn ran to intercept me, his hands steadying me. "What is it, Nhanni?"

I kept my eyes turned downward, wrapping my arms around my cold shoulders as the wind howled. *So...this entire time you've been the Oracle? You were just pretending to be my friend?*

"No! No, Nhanni! Of *course* not!"

His hand covered my cheek again. "There is a reason I want to face Raveena. Something beyond duty."

He smiled slightly, his gaze completely honest. "As the Oracle it was indeed my duty to ensure you, my only heir, would stay safe. But after I became your friend, after all those years we spent together. I broke an extremely important rule."

Which was?

"The same rule that Jael broke," he explained, looking away. "Falling in love with you."

I couldn't speak for a long time. There were no words.

O...oh...I stuttered when I could finally think again.

His jaw tightened and he slowly turned to face me. "I thought you should know. I was never pretending with you, Nhanni, and that is why Raveena has to be stopped."

You don't have to go, I said quickly, grabbing his arm when he turned away. If you're the Oracle then there's another way, and no one has to get hurt.

He stayed silent, cocking his eyebrow.

I nodded, as if to say 'trust me'. Where's Dust of the stars?

He grinned, without hesitation, stepping up to me again. "You mean you haven't figured it out yet?"

I just shook my head.

"I have been guarding the stone this whole time too," Taryn explained, lifting my hand. "The stone and it's true owner."

I gasped and stared at the small silver ring on my finger, which held a shimmering white crystal I'd worn every day since I first met him. I don't believe it...that's Dust of the stars?

"Yes. And it has been, this whole time."

I looked back up into his eyes, shaking my head. I was mad at you for giving me a priceless antique...

Taryn grinned. "That is why I could not stop laughing. At the time, you had no idea just *how* priceless it was."

How is this possible? How can I be both the Oracle and the royal sorceress at the same time?

"You cannot. The true meaning of this particular prophecy is proving very difficult for even *me* to decipher."

Taryn-

"I know you must have so many questions," he interrupted. "And I will explain everything later. But time is running out. It is your destiny to stop Raveena."

Mine? I asked in disbelief.

"Do not worry. I have seen this night a thousand times over, in dreams, crystals, and looking glasses. I know your destiny."

How can I possibly face Raveena?!

I have no power!

"As the Oracle, you will," Taryn said, with a sad smile. "It is time I passed my role onto you."

No, Taryn! Please-!

"It is alright," He said quickly, nodding with certainty and squeezing my hand. "We will see each other after. When all this is over, I will have to teach you everything I know. Remember?"

I stared for what seemed like hours and finally nodded, throwing my arms around him. I can't lose you. Do you even know what will happen when you make me the Oracle? I mean, how old are you?

"I will fade slowly. Do not worry, I will live for many years still."

I nodded into his shoulder, my eyes filling with moisture.

Taryn kissed my hair. "It is time. I must give you something precious, something you must guard at all costs. Your true name."

I took a deep breath, feeling his lips lightly brush my ear. "Your true name is...Soundless Night."

I closed my eyes; processing the words, feeling their power.

"Soundless Night," he repeated, pulling away with a smile. "It suits you, does it not?"

I nodded, sniffling pathetically.

"The sky is darkening. You must go now."

What about you? I asked, hesitantly touching his cheek.

He actually smiled and placed his hand over mine. "There is one last thing I have to do."

I grimaced. It was just like him to give me such a vague answer.

"Be strong," Taryn whispered, taking my head in his hands. "And come back to me in one piece."

I couldn't hide my gasp as he leaned forward, his lips brushing my cheek.

I could think of nothing to say.

"I am sorry…"

I summoned a nod. The moments passed long, as if we were frozen in them.

"It is time," Taryn repeated, triggering a memory so powerful that it was as if I was literally wrenched into the past. I could remember walking through many dreams. I could remember sweeping like a weightless body into the ballroom, and reaching for the crystal ball on Adriyel's desk.

I'd seen the Oracle that night.

I'd watched as he gazed into his own crystal, and saw this night, lived it, as clearly as we were living it now. Now that I knew Taryn was the Oracle, I knew that I had no reason to doubt…that so long as I followed whichever direction my heart led me, it would be the right one.

Taryn smiled as I was brought back to the present, and I released him with a soft sigh. He raised his hands, which instantly lit up with brilliant silver flames that flickered and twisted over his fingers. I gasped as Taryn blew gently over the fire, releasing a small bird made of the silver flames. It fluttered above us for a moment before soaring off into the darkness. I watched in awe, and Taryn chuckled.

What was that?

"A small measure of my power, personified."

Where did you send it? What is it for?

"It is for later. A time when my magic will be needed."

There was another silence as we both held our breath, our eyes locked as if we were mirror images of each other. At last he hugged me again, and I squeezed him so tightly his voice was strained when he asked me to let go.

"Oh, and do me one favour," he said with a smile, as he turned and disappeared into the night. "Make sure you bring Jael back with you."

Chapter twenty seven

Adriyel

"We are close," I murmured, hunched over the large map.

My eyes scanned the squiggly lines over and over, passing above the thick woods toward Windylow, then further south by Tyrone and Edelmera, then west to Whispering falls. I knew she wouldn't have left the four kingdoms, or wouldn't have gone far if she did.

One of the sorcerers shook his head and cleared his throat in the silence. "Adriyel, how did you know to track Jael instead of Raveena? What led you to believe the boy would be with her?"

I stared at the ground, sighing heavily. My breath hung in the frigid air like a small cloud, before slowly vanishing. "Lucky guess."

I glanced around at the men, huddled around the nearby fires and tents to keep warm as they waited for our next move. I could sense we were close, as if there was an invisible thread of fate guiding me, a thread that had long been tangled with Raveena's.

And with Jael's.

"What is *that*?"

I turned towards the voice. One of the men was motioning across the field from where we were camped. I quickly stepped forward, shaking my head and sighing again when I felt the rest of the men huddle behind me in fear. I blinked to clear my eyes, squinting into the darkness as the edge of the trees.

A small form came into focus, and slowly took shape as it drew closer to us. We could now see that a cloaked figure was approaching from out of the thick mist, carrying a very recognizable golden staff.

"The Oracle!" men shouted.

Everyone quickly fell to their knees, and the figure strode forward with slow steps, steps that seemed counted or choreographed as if he'd lived this moment many times over. I kept my head lowered as his light footsteps drew closer, taking a deep breath before they stopped right in front of me. When I felt his hand on my shoulder, I rose to my feet.

The Oracle pushed back his hood, and I saw it was Taryn. The men gasped, and I almost fell over in surprise.

He smiled nonchalantly. "Hello, Adriyel. I have to admit…I thought you would have found Raveena by *now*."

Chapter twenty eight

Nhanni

I love relief from not knowing.

From being too afraid to move away from the coming storm, for fear that an even greater one lies ahead. Whether a heart cowers or holds its ground, it is always haunted, always tainted, broken, and loved. Always carrying more and more weight at the end of each day.

There is a time to run from the unknown, but also a time to face it.

If we run from every single thing that pursues us, it is true that the load we carry may not get any heavier.

But it's also true that it may not get any lighter.

I was ready to face the unknowns, to face fear.

There's something oddly magical about flying when you're scared of heights. I don't think anyone's really scared of heights, they're just scared of falling.

There's a reason falling is the most common, the most recurring dream people have. We have a way of speaking to ourselves in our dreams. The voice from the darkest depths of our hearts speaks out against the thoughts, the denials, we push into our minds.

There is always two of us.

There's the real truth we ourselves know in our own hearts, and there's the truth we convince ourselves of. There's dreams of flying, and dreams of falling. It's funny that they are seen as opposites. Is it really so impossible to think that if we kept our eyes from betraying us, both these actions would feel the same to us?

There's falling through the air and flying on it.

There is disappointment in what you have, and happiness in what you make of it. In dreams of flying there is a sense of weightlessness and freedom. I often dream of both, flying and falling, but I don't think my dreams are the point anymore.

I think facing your fear in reality, risking the chance that you may fall, is what teaches you to fly in the first place.

"Here you go," the coachman said in a bored voice, opening the door for me.

I closed my journal before glancing up and nodding in thanks. I quickly used a sending spell on my journal, hoping it would do what it was supposed to and appear in my bedroom, then I stepped out of the carriage into the chilly night air.

I glanced up into a surprisingly bright sky.

Full moon, I noted.

I shivered and walked up the steps. After a moment's hesitation, I pushed the heavy door open, peeringin.

I met no resistance; it all seemed too easy. I stepped through the door, my fist clenching and unclenching at my side. I rounded the corner, and came into a long, dimly-lit room. The one from my dream, and the visions I'd seen over the past several months.

There were still large mirrors pushed up against the walls and the room was lit by the hugest fireplace I'd ever seen, flickering with deep-purple flames. There was something ominous about the place, I could hear a soft crying sound, small whispering voices from beneath the floor and behind the walls.

Raveena, who was staring intently at the surface of a mirror, turned around at the sound of my footsteps.

I grimaced. *Déjà vu.*

Jael appeared behind her, his eyes even wider than hers. *"Nhanni?"*

He took one step towards me and Raveena whirled to face him with an angry glare.

He slowly backed away. I know *I* would have.

"You!" Raveena spat, her piercing green eyes wild with rage. "How can this be? What are you doing here?"

You mean I'm not good enough for you? I asked, stepping down two steps into the living room. *Sorry to disappoint.*

Raveena looked shocked, apparently unaware that I could use a *Mens Mentis Pulsus*. She spun towards the fire and I stayed silent, curious to see what she was doing. Jael watched her with a hard expression until she turned back to face me.

"Impossible! Your powers still remain sealed! How dare you even *show yourself*!"

You wanted an Oracle. Here I am.

"You honestly hope to defeat me? You're just a *child*."

Accendo! I sent fire towards her, quick as lightning.

"*Contego!*" she shouted in a panic, raising her hand and blocking my spell midair. Her eyes widened until I thought they might explode.

*Oh, it gets better...*I threw two attack spells at her, one after the other, then a trapping spell. My powers did not weaken even slightly, but I knew even *Taryn*'s incredible magic would have a limit...especially without my voice. Unlike him, I couldn't use words of power to summon advanced spells.

Raveena blocked both attacks before the trapping spell wrapped around her. She rolled across the floor then said *"Eximo!"*, jumping to her feet.

I grinned and used the invisibility spell.

She sighed angrily, her eyes darting around the room. My grin spread wider.

"Appareo! Appareo!" she shouted, throwing counter spells randomly.

I tried my best to avoid them.

After a moment she got irritated and raised her hands, palms down. *"Solum!"*

Great.

The earth shook and I toppled over, unable to hold in the 'wooosh' of air as it was knocked out of me.

"Appareo!" Her violet magic surrounded me, making me visible, and I staggered to my feet.

"Incurro!" Her attack spell hit me and I tumbled to the floor, grunting as my sore arms tried to push me back to my feet. These attack spells were much stronger than the ones I'd endured in sparring class. I couldn't summon the strength to stand. I sighed in defeat as I lay there clutching my throbbing arm to my side.

Raveena's attention was pulled from me for a moment, and I followed her gaze to see a familiar silver form come fluttering through one of the mirrors.

I recognized Taryn's little firebird immediately. I smiled as if flew in an arc and landed gently on my arm.

I stared into its glowing eyes, offering a silent thanks to Taryn for sending the bird to me. I closed my fingers around the fire. I could feel heat licking across my skin, slowly warming my body.

Raveena's expression hardened as I stood, and she hastily reached towards the tall fireplace. She kept her eyes on me as fire accumulated in her palm, and when it grew to a massive size she directed it straight at me. I grinned, unafraid of the violet flames speeding towards me, and pushed my palm forward at the last moment.

The flames where deflected in a giant dome, towering over Raveena's head and making her eyes widen in horror. The dome of fire then separated into more firebirds, circling the room at top speed before spiraling towards Raveena. As they landed on her, they set fire to her clothing, making her screech and mutter spells between clenched teeth as she swatted at the flames.

I stared in wonder for a moment, gripping my limp left arm.

Her expression changed. "*Advoco!*"

A tall black staff appeared in her hand, and she smiled at me before hitting it against the floor. "*Aqua.*"

A hole opened in the floor. Around the staff, foamy green water came sloshing out in giant waves, speeding forward at top speed.

Oh no...she knows.

I screamed as the giant waves approached me, and noticed that Jael blinked, as if freeing himself from a trance. "Nhanni!"

The water surrounded me and I quickly clamped my mouth shut, trying my best to push myself towards the surface the way Taryn had shown me. I was tossed around like a limp doll, and then just floated uselessly. I couldn't move an inch. Then, just as quickly, the water slid out from under me as it vanished into thin air.

I tumbled to the floor, coughing and gasping.

"*Exitium!*" came Jael's voice as he ran past Raveena, his arms circling me and his eyes staring down at me in horror.

"Stupid girl!" Raveena screeched, raising her hand. "You've awakened him!"

Jael pulled me to my feet, but then made the mistake of meeting Raveena's eyes.

"*Mentem controlare*" she recited.

"*Sino mea oculos factus vos conspectus.*
Sino mea vox laevo in tamen ad is sonor."

No! Don't!

"*Vos occulta timor mos cedo is verum.*
Ad tento vos pedes ad currere de sui propila."

NO!

Jael's face had already gone blank, his eyes staring at nothing, and I quickly shot a petrifying spell at Raveena as she strode forward. She would not be able to counter the spell herself, but I knew that it didn't last long.

Jael, look at me! Look at me! I pleaded, taking his head in my hands and making him face me. *Give me your true name, Jael. I have to free you from her.*

He stared blankly.

Remember I said softly.

I stood on my toes, kissing him lightly. *Remember.*

I stared into his eyes until, at last, he blinked again. "Nhanni?"

We don't have much time, Jael. Raveena won't stay frozen for long. Please, give me your true name. You can trust me.

He quickly glanced at Raveena, then back at me.

Raveena gasped and took several steps forward, her lips curled into a snarl. "Meddling fool!"

Jael quickly pulled me to him, pressing his lips to my ear. "My true name is…" he whispered softly. "Tear of sun."

"Jael!" Raveena called, moving towards us. "Finish her off!"

Exsuscito I thought in my mind, hoping desperately that the spell worked.

Jael turned away from me slowly, and approached the fireplace with heavy steps, like he was sleepwalking. Raveena grinned as he raised his hands toward the flames, the medallion around his neck glowing with vibrant light. They flickered wildly, growing and glowing more brightly. The soft whispers grew louder, reaching a crescendo until they rang in my ears like reverberating bells.

At the last moment Jael whirled around. "*Incurro!*"

Caught by surprise, Raveena was hit with his spell and fell to the floor. It gave Jael just enough time to spin back, grab a clear crystal ball off the mantle, and smash it at his feet.

"NO!" Raveena cried.

Blue light exploded from the broken glass, flooding the room and forcing me to shield my eyes. As the magic danced about the room the whispers became voices that chanted and sang, as if glad to be free. The light snaked around my legs, circling me before quickly entering my body through my mouth.

I felt I should choke. Or scream.

Finally, when the light had completely entered my body and I could finally breathe again, I fell to my knees, panting.

"Nhanni?!" Jael said, running from the fireplace with a worried expression.

I staggered to my feet. "I'm fine."

He stopped abruptly, staring at me in surprise.

I gasped when I saw the familiar light return to his eyes, and stood speechless for what felt like an eternity. A smile slowly began to spread across my face as I realized what had happened.

"*More* than fine," I clarified, touching his cheek and releasing a relieved sigh. "I can…*speak.*"

Chapter twenty nine

Raveena rose clumsily to her feet, panting and eyeing Jael furiously. Both of us stiffened and turned towards her with our hands raised.

Jael pushed me behind him. "Don't interfere, Nhanni."

"But-"

He turned to face me, his eyes flashing. "She's *mine*."

I blinked in surprise.

He faced Raveena again, his arm shooting out and sending an attack spell towards her. Then another. I caught a breath as I watched, shocked that he was casting spells without words of power. Raveena stumbled back, frantically dodging his attacks. She tried her best to knock them aside with her tall staff, at the same time she attempted to get as far away from him as possible.

"*Accendo!*" she called, sending violet fire towards him at the speed of light.

Jael brushed the spell aside, almost easily, raising his other hand. "*Destineo.*"

Following the movement of his hand, Raveena was yanked off the floor and pinned against the wall. She coughed and gasped, frantically kicking her legs in the air, as Jael slowly crossed the room towards her.

"Jael-"

"Go, Nhanni! While you have the chance!"

"But-"

I was interrupted by a violent explosion of light. I shielded my eyes. Robed figures appeared from one of the enormous mirrors, melting through the smooth glass surfaces as easily as if they were walking through walls of water. The shadows glided gracefully into the room as Jael and I watched in astonishment.

When the light finally died down, I opened my squinted eyes to see that there were probably more than thirty sorcerers in the room now, all wearing the familiar deep blue banners around their arms.

The Royal Army...well some of them at least.

"Adriyel!" I called, when I noticed him at the front of the group. I noticed Taryn next to him as well, and my smile widened even more. "Taryn!"

Both of them approached me when they heard my voice, their expressions frozen in shock.

"W-what-? I mean...h-how?" Adriyel stuttered.

"I see," Taryn said, smiling brightly at me. "You managed to break the seal. You released your powers *and* your voice."

"Not me."

I glanced at Jael and, though he still had Raveena pinned against the wall, he met my gaze. "Him."

Raveena struggled even more against Jael's hold, staring at Adriyel and the Army in shock.

"Jael, take Nhanni and get out of here, *now*. The Army and I will take things from here."

"No!" he replied

Adriyel blinked in surprise. "*What*?"

"I'm staying! Do you have any idea what she-?"

"Taryn explained everything," Adriyel said calmly, eyeing Raveena. "Rest assured, she will pay heavily for all she has done. She will no longer be a threat to anyone."

Jael kept his eyes on Raveena, his jaw clenched and his eyebrows pulled together.

"Jael, please."

Jael finally relaxed, turning to meet Adriyel's gaze.

Adriyel nodded and raised his hands toward Raveena. "Do not even try to escape, Raveena. The rest of the Army has this building completely surrounded."

Jael lowered his hand, and immediately, she toppled to the floor.

Taryn turned to me as Jael approached us, pushing a scroll of some kind into my hands. "This map will lead you to the palace. You and Jael must get there as quickly as possible, and *stay* there until we know Raveena has no other allies."

"You can't be serious?" I said in disbelief. "*You're* going to stay here when you're completely *powerless*?"

"You are mistaken. I still have some magic in me."

"That's not the point!" I muttered furiously, while Jael watched us argue with a surprised expression. "Adriyel said himself that they would have a better chance of defeating Raveena with the Oracle's help. *I'm* the Oracle now! I have my power *and* yours. I can help!"

Taryn just sighed, but Jael glanced at me in horror. "*You* want to *fight*? Who are you, and what have you done with Nhanni?"

I folded my arms over my chest with an angry groan.

We heard cries from the living room. Turning back, we saw that Raveena was making good use of the mirrors lining the walls. There appeared to be several fire attacks bouncing back and forth across the room. Adriyel and the Army did their best to counter and avoid them.

"Adriyel!"

"He is fine, Nhanni! You have to leave!"

"I think he's right, Nhanni," Jael added, taking my arm and trying to pull me away with a worried expression. "Raveena may try to steal your powers again. We can't risk it. You're new to being the Oracle and you don't know the full extent of your power. Raveena knows *twice* as many spells as you."

"Taryn!" One of the sorcerers called. We all turned towards him. "Get in there! Adriyel's not looking so good!"

He motioned to the far end of the room, where Raveena and Adriyel were locked in an attack and defense battle.

Taryn jumped into the fray, and naturally I followed him.

Jael of course, followed *me*. "Nhanni!"

We all ran forward, just as Adriyel was sent flying backward in an explosion of light.

"Adriyel!" Jael and I called.

"*Absconditus!*"

All at once, we turned our heads towards the front of the room just in time to see Raveena vanish.

"Stay alert, everyone! Nobody move or speak, listen closely for her movements!" Adriyel commanded. When he silence, the room was deathly quiet.

Taryn and Jael stood on either side of me, their eyes scanning the room quickly.

"Did she escape?" Jael finally whispered.

Taryn spun around, his eyes resting on the floor just behind me. "Nhanni!"

He ran forward and covered me with his arms, making a strange, strangled sound.

I realized he was hurt, and my breath turned to stone inside me. "Taryn!"

Taryn toppled over as Jael cried. "*Appareo!*"

Adriyel ran to help Jael fight Raveena, while everyone else huddled around me and Taryn.

"Taryn?" I said again, my eyes watering.

His eyes were closed, but as I watched they opened and stared at me with a confused expression. "Umm...I'm okay."

"What?"

He sat up slowly, his eyebrows pulled together in thought, and I glanced at his back to see the knife wound there slowly closing.

I stared at him in shock. "How are you doing that?"

His expression suddenly softened, a look of realization crossing his face. "It is not me...it is *you*."

"*What*?" I asked again.

"Incredible...you are using your powers without being conscious of it. Healing powers. That's new."

Taryn glanced towards the front of the room, where Adriyel and Jael were fighting Raveena together. He swiftly got to his feet.

"I am afraid I will have to channel some of your power, Nhanni," he said, taking my hand and dragging me behind him. "It is time to put an end to this."

He ran full-speed towards Raveena, with me tripping and stumbling behind him, trying to keep up. Raveena had Adriyel and Jael pinned to opposite sides of the room, both her arms raised to keep them there.

Taryn held out his hand. "*Advoco!*"

A staff came flying through one of the mirrors, and caught it out of the air. It was a beautiful staff: two coils of solid gold wrapped around each other and a shimmering purple stone at the top. Taryn threw a spell at Raveena, who, fortunately for us, had her hands full. She dropped her arms and quickly brushed the spell aside.

Adriyel and Jael both fell to their feet, gasping.

Taryn continued to attack Raveena, and I ran to help them. "Jael!"

I threw my arms around him, almost knocking him over, but he didn't seem to mind. His arms circled me protectively as we both glanced towards Taryn. Raveena was backed up against the fireplace, with nowhere to run. Taryn stood before her with his staff raised.

"*Vacuo*," Taryn recited, his eyes closing.

"No!" Raveena pleaded, shaking her head wildly.

"Parvos manus obnatus et pertingens.
Ita vos queo discere cunctum re denuo."

While Taryn quietly recited the spell, everyone in the room fell silent and stared in wonder. There were tiny figures leaping from the flames, human-like figures made of fire that danced around the room like walking suns.

"Is canticum cecineruntque re et re

Ad admoneo vos de quails est verus."

The flames circled Raveena, dancing around her and singing, almost as if joining in Taryn's chant. Raveena cried out, clutching her head and clenching her jaw.

After a moment, Taryn opened his eyes, motioning towards Raveena with his staff. "*Vacuo.*"

"NO!" she shrieked.

The flames ran towards her, creating a harsh light as they joined together into a single orb of light, with Raveena at the core. After only a second, the figures burst out from Raveena again, skipping jovially back into the tall fireplace. The flames lost their human shapes and grew to fill the hearth, flickering in orange tendrils and exploding small sparks. The fire no longer glowed with a violet light. Raveena stood motionless at the front of the room, tears slowly streaming down her face.

"Take her into custody," Adriyel instructed, and two sorcerers quickly pinned her arms behind her back and dragged her toward the doors.

I glanced at Jael, and we both ran toward Taryn at the same time.

"What happened?" I asked. "Is it over?"

"Yes," Taryn replied.

He lowered his staff, turning to us with a relieved smile. "The Army is taking her to the palace prison. She cannot harm anyone else. And she will not be released for a long time, I imagine. Maybe never."

"But, this is *Raveena* we're talking about," Jael added. "She'll definitely find a way to escape from a prison cell. That should be *easy* for her, even if it's a magical prison."

"She will not escape. Do not worry."

"She's very powerful, she took on both Adriyel and the Army at once," I said. "How do you know, Taryn?"

"Because, all of her powers are gone now."

Chapter thirty

I eyed the fancy carriage nervously, while Adriyel and Taryn spoke with some of the sorcerers who were still at Raveena's cottage. It was hard to believe our enduring conflict with her was finally over. For some reason, I didn't feel a thousand times safer. I felt stronger, yes, but my newfound power frightened me, as well as the responsibility left to me by Taryn now that I was to become the Oracle. The carriage was here to take all of us to the safe borders of the palace. The *palace*…the place I would be living for the rest of my life.

Jael came up to me, laughing. "You can relax, Nhanni. It's okay." I glared, and he laughed again as his arms circled me. "She's gone. For good. Everything's going to be okay."

"How do you know?"

He cocked his eyebrow. "*You're* the Oracle. You tell me."

My eyes narrowed and I glanced down with a sigh.

"Maybe we haven't had our fill of fighting, and there's going to be a lot more struggle down the road," Jael finally said after a moment. I glanced up again. "But you're safe and we have one less enemy than we did before. Now that I think of it, everything might not be okay after all."

He smiled, brushing a lock of red hair from my eyes and leaning forward. "Everything's going to be *better* than okay."

I closed my eyes and gave in, kissing him back. It wasn't long before we heard a disgusted grunt, and turned towards the carriage to see Taryn glancing in our direction.

"Get a room."

"Who asked you to watch?" Jael muttered.

"Now, now." Adriyel sighed, appearing from behind us. "Not *this* again…"

I smiled at him. "So, what now Adriyel?"

"Well Taryn, for obvious reasons, passed his role onto you before you were ready, so you will have to complete your training with him before you officially accept the role as the Oracle. The ceremony will be postponed until you're ready."

"And what about the prophecy?" Taryn asked. "It still does not make any sense, even to *me*. I always thought that it spoke of Nhanni, and that is why I gave the ring to her. But it appears I was mistaken."

Jael glanced at my ring. "*What*? That's *Dust of the stars*?"

Adriyel nodded. "Yes, but there is no way Nhanni can be the royal sorceress *and* the Oracle. It appears the prophecy has not come true yet."

I stared at the ring a long time, and then it all made sense. "The ring still hasn't been given to its rightful owner…"

All three of them glanced at me, and I grinned.

"Ever since you gave me the ring, Taryn, I was meant to pass it on to the true owner, the person who would become royal sorcerer."

I pulled the ring off my finger. "*Incrementum.*"

The silver band of the ring grew larger, large enough to fit on a boy's finger.

Adriyel gasped as I grabbed Jael's hand, placing the ring in his palm. "It is destiny. I was meant to give it to you all along."

Jael stared at the ring, his mouth open.

"Whoa," Taryn said, his eyes wide. "Even *I* did not see that coming..."

*****

"It is decided," Adriyel beamed. Jael stared at the ring on his finger. "Jael, you will come to the palace as well to complete your training with me. Who knew that all along *you* were the true subject of the prophecy, even though Taryn thought he was just tricking Raveena..."

We were all loading huge bags of belongings into the back of the carriage, preparing for life in a huge palace. We had come to The Academy, and grabbed all our things after we left Raveena's cottage.

"I still don't understand everything that's happened," I admitted, glancing at Taryn.

"Neither do I," a familiar voice murmured.

We all spun around, and I flashed a smile. "Dad!"

He was just stepping out of a carriage. He laughed as I ran toward him and hugged him tightly.

"Adriyel said that your voice had returned, but I'm not sure I actually believed it until now. It's just so...different."

I smiled. "Are you coming too?"

"Of course, Nhanni. I couldn't live so far away anymore, especially now that prophecies are coming true one after the other."

Adriyel shook his hand and sighed. "I believe it is about time we explained everything to you," he said to me and Jael.

"You mean...this whole thing with Raveena?"

He nodded. "As you know, when you were very young, Nhanni, Raveena feared you would become royal sorceress and stole your voice to weaken your power."

I nodded for him to continue.

"I knew already that you would be my successor," Taryn put in. "But I also believed you to be the subject of my prophecy. And so, when the prophecy became known, I told Raveena that it was about Jael instead."

Adriyel nodded. "But this plan backfired. Raveena learned your true name, Jael, and took you from your real parents when you were still an infant."

Jael's eyes widened. "What?"

"I am sorry you did not find out till now. But Raveena has known your true name all this time. She has been controlling you your entire life, and you never knew it."

"Raveena was smart," Taryn said. "She knew the chances of you helping her get what she wanted would be higher if you were under the impression that she was your mother."

"We were lucky," he said with a smile, turning to me. "Nhanni awakened you, and then broke the spell."

"So..." Jael said, looking bewildered. "Raveena is not my real mother?"

"No," Adriyel replied.

Jael glanced at Adriyel, then at Taryn, then at Adriyel again. "Then...who are my real parents?"

Taryn nodded to Adriyel, who took a deep breath and stepped forward. He smiled as he awkwardly placed a hand on Jael's shoulder. "I suppose you are going to have to get used to calling me *dad*."

Chapter thirty one

That night was our first night at the palace.

I stepped into my enormous room, and it echoed with the slightest sound. It smelt strongly of expensive perfumes. I was almost twice as intimidated as when I faced Raveena for the first time. I found it hard to fall asleep once I was curled under the soft sheets. There is something comforting about familiarity, about the place we call home, and I knew it would take some getting used to...calling the palace home.

But at last, I did drift off into sleep. My mind spun beautiful dreams rather than the nightmares that had haunted me for so long. Overcoming fear the first time is the hardest, I realized. But the more fears you face, the easier they are to overcome in the future. And I was ready.

I slept through the whole night.

It wasn't until the first rays of morning light began to seep through my window that I woke to the sound of soft, padding footsteps coming through my open door. My mind resisted, trying to stay under, and I sighed and tried to fall back asleep rather than open my eyes.

I heard an annoyed 'huff', and I groaned as something light landed on my stomach. *"What?"*

I could only make out a soft humming noise, almost purring, and I could feel soft vibrations against my stomach where the light weight was still resting.

Something tickled my nose.

"Fine..." I sighed, blinking my tired eyes open and stretching my arms over my head. "This better be good-"

I stopped short. I blinked sleep from my eyes and I watched a small white tail flick playfully back and forth. The animal was crouched on my stomach, its wide green eyes staring into mine from inches away, its whiskers lightly brushing my cheeks. I took a moment and tried to decide whether this was a dream or reality.

"You're a...cat." I muttered as I sat up.

The cat's eyes narrowed, and I could almost hear a sarcastic voice saying *"Oh really?"*.

"Were did you come from?" I asked, as if the cat could answer, and glanced towards my open door. "And why did you come *here*? Don't you have an owner somewhere?"

Those cat's unblinking eyes continued to stare, and I sighed to myself as its furry tail continued to flick. Something about this cat struck me as different...human-like. But I quickly decided it was likely sleep or my imagination still playing tricks on my mind. "Run along now, cat. I'd like to get a bit more sleep tonight."

I hoped the cat would understand what I was asking and find a different bed to occupy, preferably a bed in one of the many empty rooms lining this hall. The cat didn't, but sank lower and dug its claws into my thick sheets.

I cocked my eyebrow. "Oh, you've got an attitude? Not a chance. Up you go, kitty." I gently lifted the cat off of me and placed it on the floor beside my bed. "Run along, now."

My eyes closed once again, and I pulled the sheets back over me with a relieved sigh. My mind almost slipped into unconsciousness, when I felt a 'thud' against my stomach again.

"*Why?*" I groaned, lifting my head. "What? What do you *want?*"

Well first of all…don't scream. No one can hear us. And no one can know what I am about to tell you.

At first I didn't know if I'd just imaged the soft female voice that drifted into my head. But, as the cat continued watching me expectantly, my mouth dropped open."Did you…did you just-?"

Yes. Remember what I said, Nhanni. No one can hear us. You must use your Mens Mentis Pulsus when you speak with me.

There was something calming about her voice. It was as if I'd heard it before, perhaps in a dream or some long-forgotten memory.

Please. The information I bring is important.

O-okay…

I've been at the palace for a while, but I lived in Windylow for most of my life before I came here. There are certain planned events that will soon be taking place…events that your king and your prince know nothing about.

So why have you come to see me? I asked.

As the soon-to-be Oracle, it will be your duty to protect the royal family. There will be a time when we will have to rely on each other to restore peace and balance between the kingdoms.

I sat up once again, transfixed by her piercing green eyes. *Something will happen to shake the peace we took so long to achieve? And you want to ally yourself with me? How do you know our loved ones will support our agreement when the time comes?*

I know it is a lot to ask... but for the time being it would be best if we kept this between us. We have no way of knowing the exact moment these events will take place, but I do know that if we can't rely on our own kingdoms to try and find balance, we must rely on our own strength.

I couldn't help but smile as I sat in silence a moment, shivering in the cold air of the giant bed chamber. *Not to be rude... but may I ask how you will be of help to me when this time comes?*

I jumped in surprise as the fireplace sparked to life across the room, burning with brilliant light and emanating wonderful heat. The cat's wide eyes glimmered in the soft orange glow, and my heart started to pound as I turned to her again. Now that I could see more clearly, her furry tail caught my attention once again. Before I'd thought her tail was just flickering abnormally fast, but now I could see that her tail was actually glowing with its own light, light like flames.

You're...a Snow Falene. I've only ever read about creatures like you in myths.

It is true that our dwindling numbers have made the gene quite rare, but there are still some in this world. And the extent of our powers has not yet begun to weaken.

A loud sound from somewhere in the palace made both of us glance towards my door, and the cat quickly jumped from my bed and padded towards the light coming from the hall.

"Wait!"

The cat stopped at the sound of my voice, turning back to look at me.

"Mistwalker..." I whispered softly, remembering that I was not supposed to wake anyone. "That is your name, isn't it? Your true name."

I thought I saw her small mouth tilt up into a smile. *You are the young Oracle, Nhanni. You tell me.*

"Tell me Mistwalker...do I know you?"

No, she replied with a purring voice, as she retreated back through the door. *But you will.*

Chapter thirty two

Adriyel

It was past nightfall, and Jael, Nhanni, and Taryn were all sleeping soundly within the safe borders of the palace. It was as if a weight had been lifted off my shoulders. A sense of relief filled me the moment they stepped through the doors. I felt almost weightless, free. There were no more threats, and nothing to shake the peace and security the people of Arhyenia were starting to regain.

I waited until I could hear Jael's soft snoring from next door before I slipped from my chamber. I didn't bother wearing a cloak or hood as I made my way to the stables, as I was more likely to attract attention that way. It was safest to pretend I was supposed to be wandering the halls in the dead of night.

I came outside, and stepped into the small shack to shake the grumpy coachman awake.

When I told him where I was headed, he mumbled so sluggishly I wasn't certain he was even awake yet. It wasn't till I dangled a small sack of coins in front of his face that he jumped to his feet. He saddled the horses and prepared the coach as quickly as he could, and within moments we were riding down the road leading away from the palace.

I remained silent as we rode on, and thankfully the coachman didn't bother me with questions or warnings. It wasn't till we reached the tall stone building and came to a halt that he simply muttered that he would wait for me there. The guards at the doors seemed surprised to see me, but didn't say a word and tried to avoid meeting my gaze as I passed.

I stepped silently through the halls, like a shadow, until I reached the base of the winding stairs. I could see nothing but darkness stretching above me, and I grabbed one of the torches from the wall before slowly making my way up to the tower. I could hear quiet dripping as I took slow steps up, and the creaking of floorboards and chairs downstairs as guards shifted uncomfortably from sitting for so long. I reached the top, where another guard blinked sleepily as I neared with the bright torch.

"I just need a moment."

"Oh, it's you Adriyel. Go ahead."

I nodded thankfully and turned the corner, making my way to the very end of the hall. I held the bright light close to the row of iron bars.

"What do *you* want?" Raveena hissed.

I followed the sound of her voice, dry and raspy from lack of water, and finally spotted her in the corner where her eyes reflected moonlight seeping through a small window.

"I want to know what happened to you, Raveena. What caused such a magnificent sorceress like you to be brought so low?"

Her lips pulled up into a smile as she continued gazing longingly at the night sky. "I always knew you would be the death of me, Adriyel."

"You should count your blessings that your life was spared once again. I was not expecting The Oracle to be as forgiving as I was, even after I found out it was Taryn. Do not feel bitter towards him. He had every opportunity, and every right, to kill you."

"He may as well have. I will not consider any of the days spent in this place as a day spent living. I am nothing without my powers. It was the only good quality my master, Danton, ever saw in me, the only good quality *anyone* ever saw in me."

"I saw good in you, Raveena. You know I did," I placed the torch in a holder on the wall, and crouched closer to the bars. "To me, there were so many wonderful things about you, not just your magic. In fact, I was beginning to see that it was your only *bad* quality. You are just like Jael used to be, you know. You were both seen as selfish and power hungry. You overlooked the fact that as long as you were happy with who you were…the opinions of others would not matter."

"I never cared what they thought," she muttered, turning to me with dark eyes.

"Yes, you did. People continued to say things about you that, sooner or later, you knew you would start to believe.

The only thing they admired about you were your powers, and you became so obsessed with rising above everyone else in order to please them that you did not even realize you were tearing them down to do it."

"I don't want your words of wisdom now, Adriyel. Or your pity."

I shuffled forward, but stopped when she flashed a warning glance. "I wouldn't do that if I were you...this entire cell is enchanted. I'm not entirely sure what will happen if you even *touch* those bars, but I'm sure you don't want to find out."

Heeding her warning, I shuffled back and took a seat on the cold ground. "It is never too late for you to try to be her again, the better version of you. She is still inside you somewhere. No matter how deep you have buried her...she can still be found."

Raveena's eyes stared out through the window again. She remained silent, showing no sign of having heard what I said.

"We were once friends, Raveena," I began again, my voice lowering automatically as if the very walls might repeat our secrets. "Do you think we can ever be those people again?"

"No," she said simply, her voice only a barely audible whisper. "No, I don't think we can."

"It is never too late. The girl I knew at The Academy...she is still a part of you. I know it."

"You're wrong."

I smiled slightly, shaking my head at her and rising to my feet. "When have I ever been wrong, Raveena?"

"You were wrong about me *then*," she muttered, risking a glance in my direction. "And you're wrong about me now."

I sighed heavily. I was beginning to think it really was hopeless, and there was just no way to get through to her anymore. "You know…I am trying to give you a second chance, Raveena. But you are making it fairly difficult."

"I told you already. I don't want your pity, or your help. I don't need it. I'm done."

"You are done? Done what, exactly? Pretending?"

Raveena's whole body tensed, and rage filled her eyes as she pushed herself to her feet. "What do you mean 'pretending'?"

"Pretending like you do not care…like you do not wish you could take back all those years you spent terrifying and harming others for no reason?"

"No reason! You think I had *no reason*? You truly are that oblivious, aren't you?"

Her anger startled me, and I couldn't help but take several steps back from the cell. Her eyes rested on mine expectantly, and I kept my voice calm as I spoke again. "What are you talking about, Raveena?"

"I'm taking about all those years we were friends, all those years that you stood up for me, only for you to forget about me when you fell in love with that *stupid* girl!"

"Is that what you think? That there was no more room for you in my life after I fell in love? You were my friend, Raveena, and just because I started caring about somebody else did not mean I stopped caring about you."

There was a long pause as her eyes fell, and she slowly sank back to her seat on the cold floor. I watched her with water in my eyes, but she refused to meet my gaze again.

"This is the real reason you have hated me all these years? You really thought so highly of me when we were in school?"

"Is that so hard to believe, Adriyel?"

I released a deep breath to break the silence, and moved slowly back towards the torch as it gave off a small amount of heat. I grabbed the torch from the holder, and was about to leave when Raveena's voice stopped me.

"Adriyel?"

I turned back, and she'd finally looked away from the small window. Her eyes glistened with moisture, which she quickly wiped away as I approached the cell. "I never meant to hurt her."

"I know."

She stared, her face glowing with the bright light of the flickering fire. I nodded, and a small smile spread across my lips. "I know…and I forgive you."

"Don't."

"What?" I asked in confusion.

"Just don't. Please."

"Why?"

"Because I don't want you to."

I stepped closer to the cell when she shuffled away, heat rising to her cheeks again. "You can't just forgive me so easily! You can't possibly think of me as a friend after what I did to her, and to everyone else! It's a trick! You're not here to make amends...you're here to get information out of me!"

Raveena continued shrieking even when I tried to speak out in protest, her eyes wild with rage. Her tears dried just as quickly as they'd formed. I watched her a while longer, my face falling as the old Raveena slowly slipped away again.

I turned back towards the exit, shaking my head. "The Army and I have no more quarrel with you, Raveena. I have offered you a second chance, but you have refused to take it."

Raveena silenced abruptly, and she ran to the edge of her cell when I started to leave. "Adriyel!"

"Do not expect me to return. Apparently, I came here in search of someone who no longer exists. Enjoy your days in that cell."

"How dare you-!"

"You do not fool me anymore. It was cruel for you to use me this way, to manipulate me, and play with my emotions as if you were plucking the strings of an instrument! Your days of taking advantage of people, and using their weaknesses against them, are over. Your powers are gone for good, and now there is no way for you to get what you wish."

She stood on the other side of the bars, her eyes radiating fury, and her hand clenching into a fist at her side. I got the feeling that she knew I was going to come…that she was somehow relying on it to find a way to escape. She knew that our past friendship left me with a soft side for her, a side that constantly hoped she would see the good in herself, the good that I used to see in her.

"I will not end my days in this prison!" she declared, shouting although her voice was hoarse. "I will find a way to get out, and I will find you, and that meddling girl, again! Do not make the mistake of thinking I can beaten so easily!"

"Oh, but you have been beaten, and by three apprentices not unlike ourselves all those years ago. They did everything you could not do: let go of their desires for acceptance, their hatred, and their fear. They moved past all of their hardships, they got past all of your attempts to tear them apart, and now are even closer because of all that has happened. Their bonds of love and friendship are stronger than your bitterness and hatred…stronger than your magic ever was."

I turned and strode down the hall, without looking back. "Give it up, Raveena. It is over now."

"It's not over!" she called behind me, her voice ringing through the halls. "Not even close!"

Chapter thirty three

Three months later

I don't find it hard to remember a dream anymore, not now that I've noticed a small light creeping through the darkness. The light had always been there, the epiphany, but this was the first time I had seem it clearly.

Maybe I had always seen it, just never believed in it. There is beauty in all things, and hope, and light, as long as you look hard enough. As long as you learn to see and traverse past the unfortunate, the hideous tragedies that trick us into believing they will become us.

That they will define us for eternity.

It is the good that should become us, that will. It is the bravery, the wisdom, the loveliness, and the justice that will write our histories and our ambitions. Maybe then what we know to be universes out of reach can become a possibility, and all it would take is a small leap of faith.

I was ready to remember beauty, and to treasure it, to acknowledge the mistakes and to regret them, to trust my view of good for what it is and to follow it. I was ready to speak without words, to say what was meant to be said through my movements, my actions.

Though I knew there would be dangers, losses, disbeliefs, and disregards, I knew fighting and losing was a step up from drowning in my fears. I knew now that reaching through the ocean's blurred void gave me a higher chance of grasping land that allowing the waters to swallow me.

I knew more with uncertainty than with knowledge.

It is better to be uncertain about one's success, than sure of one's failure. I was ready to open my mind and my heart to life's wounds and remedies, life wisdom and hesitance, risks, victories, and failures. I was ready to speak again, after a lifetime of silence I was ready to speak out.

Make my actions my voice.

After years of cowering against the brim of my haven, balancing between a prison of calm disappointment and a world of wild and terrifying possibility, I was ready to jump. I had come to realize that not everything fades.

Even a bouquet of roses withers with time, but love is undying. It is the eternal flame of the sun, burning brightly each day, sometimes hidden by clouds, rain, and snow, sometimes eclipsed, but always there.

It brings warmth and light into days otherwise cast into shadows, the center of a circling and changing universe with no end. Larger than our world a thousand times over, larger than a billion lifetimes can hold.

Love is always there.

It is the most inexhaustible magic in our world, a figment and a truth more unimaginable than our imaginings.

It is the mystery.

The question.

The answer.

The adventure taking a lifetime to discover, but never truly explain.

Even if it is unspoken and unbearable, even if it becomes hard to see around doubt and uncertainty.

Know that it is always there.

"Nhanni!"

One of the maids opened the door, flashing a gleaming smile. "It's time," she said. "Come. You have to get ready!"

"Just a minute."

She nodded and closed the door. I turned to my journal, which was on the very last page and almost completely filled. I took my pen once again.

My mind is empty.

Empty of all the words I could never say before, empty of all the decisions I had to make and the revelations flooding my mind. Now beautifully scrawled onto the surface of lined paper.

I closed the leather cover, sighing deeply, before standing and placing the full book on my shelf. Light flooded the huge palace chamber, and I was surprised I hadn't realised it was almost noon already. Time seemed to be passing more and more quickly. Jael and I had both finished our apprenticeships here at the palace, with Taryn and Adriyel. The ceremony where I was to accept my role as Oracle was taking place very shortly.

I quickly left my room and followed the girl through the massive halls, which I still hadn't memorized, to a room just outside the grand hall. She practically shoved me through the door, where five more girls were waiting.

"Let's get her in that gown. Quick!"

I didn't stop grimacing and complaining for the next forty minutes. The dress for my ceremony seemed to have at least ten thin layers all piled one on top of the other. Just as the girls were done helping me, someone knocked on the door. All of the maids looked at each other with confused expressions before one of then finally opened the door, then stared in complete silence.

I peeked over the girls shoulder. "Taryn?"

"Well, don't you look…fancy."

My eyes narrowed.

"Pretty," he corrected. "That better?"

"You can't be here!" the girl retorted, trying to close the door on him.

He easily shoved it back open. "Just want to talk to her for a moment."

When everyone was silent, he grinned and motioned for me to follow. "Come on."

We were both quiet as he led me outside, where there were small hills covered in long grass and flowers, and lined with trees. There was a steady breeze blowing, and I breathed in the fresh air until I no longer felt like I was suffocating.

Taryn chuckled. "I know. You hate being cooped up inside for too long. They keep you like a prisoner in that palace."

"It's not so bad," I admitted, rolling my eyes. "But I could do without the long, fancy gowns."

Taryn smiled and stopped walking suddenly, and I faced him with a confused expression.

"I just wanted to wish you luck," he said. "The ceremony is simple. All you have to do is kneel before the king and accept the Oracle's staff from him.

I nodded. "Okay."

"Nhanni?"

"Uh huh?"

"*Breathe.*"

I let out a huge gust of air, making him laugh. "Do not look so nervous. You will be fine."

His eyes fell suddenly, and his face was unusually sad. "I am sorry Nhanni, but I will not be staying."

"What?" I asked, my smile disappearing.

"I have taught you all I know, and soon you will officially be the Oracle. Although I may only have a small amount of my powers left, I am still a sorcerer and I still work for the king."

I nodded slowly, my eyes falling as well. "He's given you a job to do, hasn't he?"

"Yes. I have done all I can here. It is time for me to put my powers to use elsewhere, now that the king has *you*."

"Taryn," I said softly, looking up again. "I don't want you to go."

His looked at me without saying a word, and he smiled, but it wasn't the same smile I'd seen every day since I first became an apprentice. After a moment, words came to him. "I do not want to leave, but I have to. I do not want you to worry, though. I will definitely be back."

He reached towards me and I gratefully hugged him, squeezing him tightly. "I'll miss you, Taryn."

"I know. I will miss you too."

I swallowed and held back my tears, trying my best to smile as he pulled away.

"You will not be alone. You have Adriyel. You have *Jael*. And I will be back."

I could only nod as he slowly turned away, his figure growing smaller and smaller as he neared the top of the hill.

"Taryn?"

He glanced back at me, and I managed to smile..for real. "Come back soon," I said. "And I mean *soon*. As in, not in a hundred years."

He grinned, pulling his dark hood over his head. "You got it."

*****

I was about to walk down a huge aisle of red velvet, and the only thought that came to me was, *I'm wearing a dress.*

"We're ready," one maid whispered to the other, and soon the tall doors opened and almost blinded me with light.

It was just as I imagined it: a long aisle, with several steps at the end. An aged man, who could only be the king, was waiting with Taryn's golden staff. On either side of the aisle were benches filled with people, people who had probably come from all over Arheynia. Maybe even some of the neighbouring kingdoms. I was blinded by the sunlight streaming through windows stretched from roof to floor.

"Nhanni…" the girl behind me whispered. *"Walk."*

Walk…oh…right.

I stepped forward as slowly as possible, taking deep breaths and trying not to meet anyone's gaze. The aisle felt much longer than it actually was.

Ok…just don't trip…step up one, two, three.

I made it to the top, sighing in relief and looking up with a small smile. I could hardly believe I was standing in front of the king as I looked into his small grey eyes, crinkling at the edges as he smiled.

I knelt before him, holding my hands facing up. He placed the staff, which was much heavier than it looked, in my open palms. The crowd instantly erupted into cheers. I stayed there a moment, processing that this was really happening, before standing and turning to face the endless rows of people.

Something clicked as I held the staff, looked over the crowd, and finally met Jael's gaze. He was sitting in the front row, his smile spreading wide. The crowd was still cheering, and I got Déjà vu again as I glanced at the staff, the staff I'd seen not long ago…in a dream.

Knowing now that this was all meant to be, that is was my destiny, I suddenly felt very sure.

I felt fearless.

I faced the crowd again with a confident smile, raising the staff of gold high above my head.

Made in the USA
San Bernardino, CA
24 March 2017